Awfully Short
for the
Fourth Grade

Awfully Short for the Fourth Grade

ELVIRA WOODRUFF

drawings by Will Hillenbrand

A Yearling Book

Published by
Dell Publishing
a division of
Bantam Doubleday Dell Publishing Group, Inc.
666 Fifth Avenue
New York, New York 10103

The trademark Yearling® is registered in the U.S. Patent and
Trademark Office.

The trademark Dell® is registered in the U.S. Patent and Trademark
Office.

ISBN: 0-440-40366-9

Reprinted by arrangement with Holiday House, Inc.

Printed in the United States of America

November 1990

10 9 8 7 6 5 4 3 2 1

OPM

For Noah, Jess and Nate
and Overdue, too!

E.W.

Awfully Short
for the
Fourth Grade

Chapter 1

"Yeow!" When Mr. Murphy yelled, it was usually loud. But when he sat down on the pointed helmet of Tron Man after climbing into the bathtub, he yelled very loudly.

"Yeow! Noah, get these toys out of this bathtub immediately!"

"Sorry, Dad," Noah said, rushing into the bathroom. "I guess I forgot a few." He scooped up the little men that were floating in the tub.

"Everywhere I turn, everywhere I sit, there are little men!" Mr. Murphy bellowed. "Give me patience," he moaned, as he lay back in the water.

Noah closed the bathroom door as quietly as he could. It was true; the house was full of little

3

plastic men. Noah called them his guys, and he
had been collecting them for years. There were
all kinds. There were army men, space men,
cowboys and Indians, and even cartoon figures
like He Man and Tron Man and G.I. Joe. There
were little pink wrestlers and tiny green aliens.
Noah loved them all. A lot of the kids in his
fourth-grade class had stopped playing with
them. They thought it was kid stuff. But Noah
didn't mind because his friends usually traded
or sold them to him for half price.

Noah had a lot of toys. He and his seven-
year-old brother Jess shared a bedroom. They
also shared a playroom, where they kept most of
their toys. But Noah liked to keep his guys in
shoe boxes under his bed. One night, while he
and Jess were talking in their beds, he had tried
to explain why his guys were so important.

"It's, like, it doesn't matter what happens at
school or what's happening around the house. I
can always reach into my boxes, and I know that
my guys are waiting. I can just forget everything
and have an adventure with them whenever I
want to." Noah smiled.

"Yeah, well, that's how I feel when I watch
TV," said Jess, yawning.

"TV is OK, Jess, but my guys are better

because I get to make up the adventure, and there are no commercials." Noah grinned. "Like, right now a plane is flying over enemy territory." Noah jumped off his bed and zoomed around the room with two of his favorite guys. "It's Commander Falcon and his sidekick, Sergeant Gordy. It doesn't look good for the two courageous comrades. The left wing of their plane is on fire, and the engines have quit!" yelled Noah.

Suddenly Noah switched to his Commander Falcon voice. "It's no good, Gordy; we're going to have to bail out."

"But sir, that's a mountain down there. We'll never make it!" Noah moaned in his goofy Gordy voice.

"Don't be goofy, Gordy. It's our only chance. Don't worry, old chum, I'll be right behind you," the Commander assured him.

Noah stood over Jess's bed, holding the Commander and Gordy above Jess's face. Suddenly, the two little figures came hurtling down and landed on Jess's forehead. Jess gave out a little giggle as Noah helped Gordy slide down Jess's nose.

"Well, Gordy, it was rough going there for a while, but we made it," the Commander sighed.

"Yeah, Commander, we made it all right, but this place gives me the creeps," said Gordy.

Noah stretched Gordy up to look into Jess's eyes. "And I gotta tell ya, Commander, this here is one ugly mountain!"

At this Jess burst out laughing and sat up.

"That's enough noise, you two," called Mr. Murphy from downstairs. "Remember that tomorrow is a school day. I don't want to hear one more sound, not one more peep!" he added firmly.

"Peep, peep, peep, peep." Both boys dove under their covers, laughing. They never could go right to sleep at night. Usually their mother or father had to call up and remind them several times to settle down.

"If you're not asleep by the time I count to ten, there will be no TV for a week!" Mrs. Murphy threatened.

"Oh no, Jess, she's counting again," Noah said, giggling. It seemed that Mrs. Murphy was always counting.

"If you don't clean your room by the time I count to fifteen, no one will be going out today" or "if you don't stop that arguing by the time I count to ten, no one will be getting an allowance this week, and I mean both of you!"

"Mom should get a job with the space program," Noah whispered. "She could count down for the launches."

"I can just hear her: ten, nine, eight, seven, six, five, four, three, two, one—blast off! What, you haven't blasted off yet? If you don't blast off by the time I count to ten you'll have no TV for a week, and I mean all of you!" Jess jumped over to Noah's bed and sat up with his back against the wall. Sometimes they didn't mind going to bed because they knew they could sit up talking and laughing and telling stories in the dark. Noah would open the curtains so they could look out at the moon and the stars.

It was on just such a night, when the moonlight spilled onto their blankets, that they began to talk of wishes.

"What would you wish if you only had one wish?" Jess asked, looking across the room at Noah.

"That's easy," Noah told him. "I'd wish that all my wishes would come true." Gordy and the Commander were sitting in the middle of Noah's bed, surrounded by hundreds of little pink wrestlers.

"No, that can't be a wish," Jess said as he leaned on his pillow, watching Noah.

"Well, then, I'd wish that all my guys would come to life." Noah grinned. "Wouldn't that be great?" He looked over at Jess.

"Yeah." Jess grinned back. "Then I would wish that we could shrink down to their size."

"Oh, that would be the best! Can you imagine having feet as tiny as Gordy's?" Noah held Gordy up to the moonlight. "You know, I bet you could go for years without ever changing your socks, and no one would notice because the smell would be so tiny!" He laughed.

Jess started to laugh too, but then his face grew serious.

"Is there such a thing as a tiny smell?" he asked.

Noah just groaned. Then he held up Gordy and switched to his goofy-Gordy voice.

"Well, gee, Jess, I don't know. But there is such a thing as a tiny brain, and I think yours is tinier than mine."

Jess threw his pillow across the room, just missing Noah as he ducked under his blankets. They stayed up late that night, laughing and talking about what it would be like to have their wishes come true.

Chapter 2

On Saturday morning Mrs. Murphy usually did her food shopping.

"Let's go, boys. If you're coming with me, you'd better get Overdue into his pen," she called.

Overdue was the latest addition to the Murphy household. He was a big chocolate Lab puppy with floppy ears. Jess wanted to name the pup Floppy. Noah thought it would be embarrassing to have a dog called Floppy. No one could agree on a name until the pup displayed a deep love for books, and not just any books.

"He's eating another book!" Noah yelled on the second night of the pup's arrival.

"And it's overdue," Mrs. Murphy said, shaking her head as she tried to put the ripped pages in order. Since Mrs. Murphy was a librarian, the Murphy house was full of library books. The boys had bought the puppy all kinds of doggy treats, but this pup seemed to prefer books.

"I wonder what they taste like?" Jess asked, as he licked a gardening book that the pup had dragged down from the coffee table.

"I don't know," said Noah. "But those overdue library books must really taste great, cause they're the ones he likes the best." Just then Noah's face brightened. "That's it! Overdue, Overdue Books!" And they all agreed it was the perfect name for the puppy.

Mrs. Murphy said that she was not going to stand by and let "this book-eating monster" devour one more book. (She was a true librarian at heart.) And so all of the books were placed on the topmost shelves in the living room.

Poor Overdue looked lost until he discovered something new to feast on—Noah's guys! The pup never swallowed them whole but spent a long time chewing them into little bits. Though Noah tried keeping his guys in his shoe boxes, he always managed to leave a few behind in whatever room he had been playing in. Overdue loved to squeeze under chairs or crawl behind the couch in search of these new treats.

So on Saturday morning, when Overdue was nowhere to be found, Noah suspected the worst. And sure enough, when Noah pulled back the couch in the living room, out tumbled the puppy with a guilty little bark. The headless remains of three green aliens were in a pile on the carpet.

"Will you please put your dog in his pen so we can go shopping?" Mrs. Murphy called as she put on her coat.

"OK, Mom, I'm getting him now." Noah glared at Overdue. "Bad dog, did you eat my guys?" Noah demanded. But Overdue just gave him a sweet puppy grin as if to say, "Gee, you know I wouldn't do that. I'm not that kind of dog." Noah might have believed him, but just then Overdue hiccuped and a little green alien head popped out of his mouth.

"How would you like it if someone chewed off your head?" Noah growled at the pup. "You *would* have to pick my three best aliens."

Noah reached down, picked up the three headless bodies, and put them in his jacket pocket. Jess came downstairs, and together they chased Overdue into his pen behind the garage.

In the car, on the way to the mall, Noah got out his three aliens and began to march them over to Jess's side of the back seat.

"My head, oh my head—have you seen my head?" he wailed as he made a little headless figure dance around in a circle.

"Oh, gross," Jess laughed. "Looks like a monster chewed off his head."

"That's what it was." Noah was using his little alien voice. "It was a giant fur-ball monster with sharp fanglike teeth and the worst case of dog breath I've ever come across on this planet. Now we'll never be able to get back to Saturn. Without our heads we won't be able to make contact with our mother ship."

"Don't worry, the Commander and I will come to your rescue." Suddenly Noah was using his goofy-Gordy voice. He pulled the Commander and Gordy from his other pocket.

"That's very heroic of you to offer our services, Gordy" came the Commander's voice. "But just when was the last time you made contact with someone from Saturn?"

Noah sat Gordy down on his knee.

"Well, gee, Commander, I had to say something to make him feel better. The poor little guy just lost his head!"

"You know, Gordy, sometimes I wonder just how well *your* head is attached. You should think before you open that mouth of yours. How many times do I have to tell you?" Noah turned the Commander to face the aliens.

"When did you last make contact with your mother ship?" the Commander asked.

In his squeaky alien voice, Noah replied, "Every Thursday night we send our signal, and they return it with—*yeow!*"

"Look out," called Jess as the aliens went sliding onto the floor. Mrs. Murphy had just made a sharp turn into Foodway's parking lot.

Noah scooped the aliens up and put them back into his pocket. Then he whispered to them, "We'll finish this conversation later."

Chapter 3

When they got to Foodway, Jess and Noah ran up to the toy and gum machines by the door.

"Mom, do you have a quarter?" Noah asked.

Mrs. Murphy hunted in her purse and sighed with relief when she found two quarters. Jess headed straight for the machine that had Super Balls in it. He liked to know what he was getting. Noah, on the other hand, loved surprises. He always went for the machine that had an assortment of things, like rings and whistles and tiny yo-yos. Noah put in his quarter, and a small plastic container dropped down. He grinned as he showed Jess what he had got.

"Look, it's a magic kit," he said. There was a trick penny in it along with two little cups to

15

hide the penny under, a tiny book of magic tricks, and a small pouch of silver powder.

"What's that?" Jess asked as Noah held up the pouch.

"Let me see." Noah read the instruction card. "Oh, neat, it says 'magic powder.' Stand still, Jess, and I'll turn you into a turtle!" said Noah.

"No turtles today, please," Mrs. Murphy called as she waited with her empty cart. "Come on, you two. After we finish shopping, you can each pick out a comic book."

Jess bounced his Super Ball into the store, and Noah stuffed his magic kit into his pocket. Food shopping is sort of boring, Noah thought, but at least we can go down the candy aisle and smell all the bags. (Mrs. Murphy rarely let them buy candy, but she didn't mind if they sniffed it.) So they found their way to the candy aisle and then decided to go to the pet aisle.

"Let's get Overdue a big rubber steak," Jess said as they stopped in front of the pet toys.

"Naw, that's too mean." Noah shook his head. "That would be like Mom bringing us home a big rubber pizza for supper."

"Well, how about a mouse? Overdue won't care if it's rubber or not. I don't think mice taste that good, anyway. Listen, it squeaks." Jess squeezed the mouse in Noah's ear.

"Oh, that's great. Every time he nibbles on it, he'll think the mouse is talking to him." They spent some time trying to decide what color mouse Overdue would prefer and finally settled on a bright blue one. (Even though Mr. Murphy had told them that all dogs are color blind, they held onto the hope that Overdue was different.)

On the way home Jess and Noah read the comic books they'd picked out and threw the blue mouse at each other on the back seat. As they drove down Fernwood Avenue, Noah asked Mrs. Murphy if she would drop him off at Nate Cooper's house, to play for a while. Nate and Noah had been best friends since the first grade.

"Well, all right," Mrs. Murphy agreed, as she came to a stop in front of the Cooper house. "But why don't you let your brother come along?" Jess smiled on hearing this, but Noah was scowling.

"Mom, I want to play with my friends by myself. Jess has his own friends, and I don't bother them when they want to play alone." Noah shot Jess a look that let him know how

much of a pain a little brother could be sometimes. Jess was no longer smiling, but he still had
a hopeful expression on his face.

"You know, Noah, some day you're going to
wish you had your brother close by. When you
get older . . ." Noah let out a loud sigh, inter-
rupting Mrs. Murphy's all too familiar lecture.

"I'll tell you what, Jess, when I'm a hundred
and four and you're a hundred and two, I
promise I'll stop by the old people's home and
we'll go for a few spins in our wheelchairs. But
for now could you please not come to Nate's?
Here's the mouse. You and Overdue can have it
all to yourselves." He threw the rubber mouse
into Jess's lap.

"All right," Jess said, trying to sound disap-
pointed for his mother's sake. Actually, he
didn't mind Noah's leaving since he knew his
mother would probably feel sorry for him and
let him watch cartoons. Playing with Overdue
and the new mouse was better than going to
Nate's anyway.

When the Murphy car pulled up in front of
Nate's house, Nate was sitting on his porch
steps having a serious conversation with his dog
Margo. They made a striking pair sitting there
in the sunlight, Nate's dark hair falling over his

face as he bent down to stroke Margo's shiny black coat. Nate was one of the smallest kids in the fourth grade, and Margo was one of the biggest dogs in the neighborhood. Noah smiled at seeing them together: Nate all thinness and light, Margo a massive mountain of black fur beside him.

When Nate saw Noah getting out of the Murphy car, he let out a loud "All right" and gave Noah the thumbs-up sign.

"I was just explaining to Margo that if she wants to be a really cool dog, she's got to learn to rap. All the dogs in the neighborhood are probably doing it," Nate said as he moved over on the step to make room for Noah. "Come on, Margo, don't be so bashful. Show Noah what I've taught you so far." Margo tilted her head to the side and blinked.

"I wish I had a bone to chew, or maybe just a cat or two . . ." Nate began in his huskiest Margo voice. "Being a dog, it ain't easy, sometimes it makes you queasy, when you're walking down the street in the summer and you meet a bunch of smelly feet. Oh, sure, they're in sandals or maybe flip flops, but when your nose is right there, let me tell you about the air! Well, I just gotta howl . . ." But Nate wasn't able to finish because Noah was laughing so hard that he had rolled over on top of Margo. Margo got up, trotted over to the driveway, and crawled under the Coopers' truck to take a nap.

No one could make Noah laugh as much as Nate. Together the two friends went into the Cooper house, rapping all the way. They went up to Nate's room to look at his new Winged Warrior "Vulture Man." As Noah inspected Nate's new guy, he couldn't help feeling envious. He knew Nate wouldn't want to trade him, and he knew he didn't have enough money to buy him. But he had to have him. Even just a part of him.

"Oh, Nate, this guy is the best!" Noah let out a low and hopefully pathetic whistle. "I lost my allowance for two weeks because of arguing with Jess. By the time I can save up for a Vulture Man, there probably won't be any left in the stores." Noah's shoulders slumped in despair. "How about trading Vulture Man's weapon pack for a magic kit?" he asked as he reached in his pocket.

"Well, maybe." Nate hesitated. "But just the

weapons, not the guy. Let me see the magic kit first."

Noah got the kit out but put the pouch of magic powder in his other pocket. He wanted to save the powder so he'd at least have part of the kit to play with later. Nate agreed to the trade, and while Noah inspected Vulture Man's weapons, Nate tried making the trick penny disappear.

After playing in Nate's room for a while the two boys decided to go downstairs for a snack. When they got to the kitchen, Nate searched the refrigerator for something good to eat.

"How many pickles do you want, three or four?" he asked, walking to the kitchen table with the pickle jar.

"Four, I guess. I'm kind of hungry," Noah replied. "Do you have any chocolate milk?"

Nate poured some chocolate milk into two tall glasses while Noah reached into his pocket and pulled out the three headless aliens. Nate spied the weird-looking little green bodies as he put the glasses of chocolate milk on the table.

"I know you said you were hungry, but I didn't think you'd start eating your guys," Nate said, shaking his head. "Why didn't you just ask for another pickle?"

Between gulping chocolate milk and chomping on a pickle, Noah explained how Overdue had decapitated the aliens. The two boys spent the rest of the afternoon making Vulture Man perform daring feats of magic for the little headless aliens.

Chapter 4

On Monday morning Noah and Jess got on the school bus and took the last seat. Nate usually sat across from them, but he had missed the bus, as he often did on Mondays. Nate had once told Noah that it wasn't his fault that he overslept; it was just that his body was allergic to Monday mornings.

"Jess, you move over to Nate's seat so I can dump out my guys on your seat," Noah suggested. His guys were always with him. He still had the Commander and Gordy and the little headless aliens in his jacket pocket. He pulled them all out and put them on the empty seat.

"Hey, what's this?" he wondered aloud as he

felt the little pouch. "Oh yeah, the magic powder." He grinned, holding it up.

"So what are you supposed to do with it?" Jess asked, looking over from Nate's seat.

"I don't know," Noah replied. "The writing on the package is so tiny it's hard to read. It says something about sprinkling it on me and making a wish. Wow, what if it works?"

"It's just some silver glitter." Jess shook his head. "It's like wishing on a star or believing in the tooth fairy." He was glad he was old enough now to poi..c this out because last year he had been so little he still believed in the tooth fairy.

"Why don't you wish for something good, like real food in the cafeteria instead of that rubber stuff they call spaghetti, or their green hot dogs," Jess said. He had already opened his lunch box and was eating a bag of potato chips.

"No, if it were real magic, I know just what I'd wish for," Noah said dreamily.

He was thinking about the wishes they had talked about last week. And as he sprinkled the silvery powder on the Commander and Gordy and the little aliens, he smiled, letting bits of silver shimmer on his lap. He closed his eyes and wished with all his might.

Let them all come to life, all my guys, he wished silently. And let me be their size so I can have an adventure with them.

Before Noah had a chance to open his eyes, the bus hit the bump on Black's Hill, and everyone bounced in his seat. Noah felt someone reach for his arm as he fell forward. When he opened his eyes, he expected to see Jess at his side. But when he looked, it wasn't Jess at all. It was Gordy. A full-size Gordy was sitting beside him! Gordy and the Commander were right there, smiling, moving, and breathing! Then Gordy winked at him, and Noah's mouth dropped open. In that instant he realized that his wish had come true. The Commander and Gordy were as alive as he was! With a sick feeling in his stomach Noah looked around him. A wall of brown plastic bus seat went on as far as he could see.

"It's happened! They're alive! And I've shrunk! I've shrunk down to their size!" Noah squeaked.

When Gordy sneezed, Noah almost fell off the seat with fright.

"You can even sneeze?" he gasped. At this Gordy and the Commander laughed.

"You did want us to come to life, didn't you?" the Commander asked.

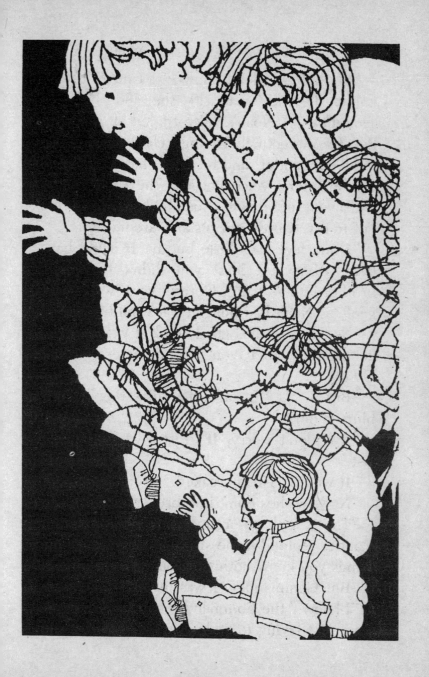

"I . . . I . . . don't know . . . I mean I *don't* know. It was just a wish, and I never thought . . ." Noah's voice trailed off in disbelief. He was actually having a conversation with the Commander, and he didn't have to use his Commander's voice because the Commander had a voice of his own. Noah bit his lip and tried not to cry. Gordy put his arm around him.

"Don't feel bad, little buddy. It could have been worse. At least you didn't turn your brother into a turtle!" Gordy's voice was just as goofy as Noah had imagined it would be.

"As far as wishes go, I think it was a pretty good one, don't you, Commander?" asked Gordy.

"But I . . . I can't stay like this," Noah blurted out.

"Aw, don't worry. It's just a wish. It won't last," Gordy said.

"It won't?" Noah croaked.

"Naw, wishes don't last forever."

"There you go again, Gordy!" the Commander scolded as he shook his head. "Saying things you know nothing about."

"But Commander, I was just trying to . . ."

"I know," the Commander interrupted. "You were just trying to make him feel better. You always want to make everyone feel better. Now let's take a hard look at the situation." He turned to Noah.

"I'm afraid my friend Gordy, for all his good intentions, has very little experience with this wishing business."

Noah's lip began to quiver.

"Of course, that's not to say he couldn't be right," the Commander hastily added.

"Let's all try and look at this thing logically. There's really no reason for panic . . ."

"I don't know about that, Commander," Gordy whispered as a giant black shadow suddenly hung over them. The three little figures looked up as a gust of wind blew against them.

"Do you smell potato chips?" Gordy yelled as his hat blew off.

"Potato chips? Yeah, you're right. That does smell like potato chips!" Noah smiled as he realized that the giant mass peering over them was a face. And that face belonged to the one person who could help them.

"I don't believe it!" came Jess's thundering whisper. "Noah, is that really you?"

Chapter 5

Looking up at Jess, even a giant Jess, suddenly made Noah feel better.

"It's me, Jess, it really is! The powder worked, and my wish came true. Look!" Noah yelled up to Jess, pointing to the Commander and Gordy.

Jess bent down closer so that he could hear the tiny figure that had once been his big brother.

"How's it going, little buddy?" Gordy called up to the towering Jess.

At the sound of Gordy's voice, Jess gasped again and dropped his bag of potato chips. All three little figures ducked as the bag narrowly missed them.

"Geeze, Jess, watch out! I'm not made of plastic, you know," Noah said.

"But Noah, you can't stay like this! What will Mom and Dad say when they see you?" Jess looked down, his eyes wild with disbelief.

"I don't know," Noah mused. He hadn't really thought about facing his parents like this. "Mom will probably take one look and start to count. I can just hear it. 'Noah, if you don't return to your normal size by the time I count to ten, there will be no allowance for a week!' " Noah laughed.

But Jess couldn't even manage a grin. He shook his head as he listened to the faint laughter that had always been so loud.

"Noah, this isn't funny. This is terrible. Why did you have to make that stupid wish? That was the worst wish!" Jess exclaimed.

"Now, let's not get excited," the Commander said. "Noah, can you remember just what it was that you wished for? I mean, the exact wish?" He looked over at Noah.

Noah looked back at the Commander. It still gave him the chills to hear that voice, the strong serious Commander's voice that he had always just imagined. He tried to think about the Commander's question.

"Well, I think that I wished that all my guys would come to life and that I would shrink down to their size," Noah said, trying not to look at Gordy, who was yawning loudly. "I can't believe you're really yawning!" Noah whispered to him.

Gordy laughed. "That's nothing," he said. "Watch this!" He leaned over and tried to stand on his head.

"Good grief, Gordy, this is no time for circus tricks," the Commander said. He turned to Noah. "What else, Noah? Can you remember anything else? We have to know the exact wish."

Noah tried to think. "No," he said. "That's all there was. I just wanted them to come alive, and I wanted to shrink so that I could have an adventure with them."

"That's it," the Commander yelled, clapping his hands.

"It is?" Gordy mumbled as he stood on his head.

"Don't you see, Noah? You only wished for all this to happen so that you could have an adventure. Since you didn't wish for anything permanent, things should return to normal once you've had your adventure." The Com-

mander ducked as Gordy came crashing down
from his head stand.

"But I'm afraid the word *normal* can never be
used in relation to my comrade here. Gordy,
have you no pride?" The Commander sighed as
he helped Gordy up.

Noah's face brightened. He was beginning to
understand just how wonderful this wish could
be..

"This could be the biggest adventure of my
life!" he thought. He looked up at his little
brother, who sat like a mountain beside him.

"Jess, we'll need your help. We can all fit in
your coat pocket. You can sneak us in," Noah
said firmly.

But Jess was looking at the front of the bus. A
first-grader had dropped his lunch box on the
floor, and everyone was jumping out of his seat
to catch the orange and cupcakes that were
rolling down the aisle.

"Sneak you in where?" Jess whispered.

"School, of course," Noah answered impatiently. "You can drop us off at my classroom.
That's where we can have our adventure." He
turned toward the Commander. "You'll like
Mrs. Adams. She's the best teacher in our
school, and she's probably the only teacher in

the whole world that has a tattoo." The Commander seemed embarrassed, but Gordy looked impressed.

"I don't know, Noah." Jess shook his head. "I don't think this is going to work."

"Why, what's the matter, kiddo?" Gordy looked up at Jess.

Jess hesitated. "Well, it's nothing personal, but you're awfully short for the fourth grade." As soon as he said it, Jess realized how funny it sounded. Noah, the Commander, and Gordy were all laughing together. In fact, they kept laughing until the bus pulled up at Roosevelt School.

"Shhh, Gordy, stop laughing. We have to get going now," Noah whispered.

"I did stop laughing." Gordy wiped his eyes. "I thought you were the one who was still laughing."

The Commander put his finger to his lips to silence everyone. With a look of horror Jess pointed to the floor. Tiny giggles were coming from beneath the potato chip bag. Everyone looked down and listened as the tiny squeaks of alien laughter grew louder!

Chapter 6

"Oh my gosh!" Noah was the first to say anything. "The aliens! They were on my lap when we hit the bump. When I made my wish, I said all my guys. I wished for all my guys to come to life!"

"Oh no," groaned Gordy. "Not the headless ones, too!" They stared at the quivering potato chip bag. No one moved. Finally the Commander straightened up.

"All right, let's look at this thing logically. We've a rather unique situation here, but there's no need to panic. What is important is that we act fast."

He was right. The bus doors had opened, and the children in front were beginning to file out.

36

"Go ahead, Jess. The Commander's right. Just reach down and pick them up, quick." Noah tried to sound as courageous as he could.

"Me?" Jess looked horrified. "I can't! They're headless!"

"Headless but harmless," the Commander said.

"Just try and think of them as they were, when they weren't real," Noah suggested.

"Easy for you to say." Jess closed his eyes and lifted the potato chip bag. There on the floor lay the three green aliens. They looked exactly as they had when Noah bought them at Kramer's Toy Store, except now they had no heads.

"Well, as long as they don't move, I guess I can . . ." Jess quickly reached down for them.

"Oh, gross!" he yelled, as they began to squirm and wiggle in his hand. He hurriedly dropped them onto the seat.

The biggest alien stood up and scrambled over to Gordy. "Hail, oh mighty and magnificent earthling. We meet again!" He bowed to Gordy. But since he didn't have a head, just his little green chest bent down. Gordy returned the bow.

"Well, little buddy, you may not be very pretty, but you sure have taste. Yeah, you know

I've been called that before. Mighty magnificent, that's me . . ."

"Not now, Gordy," the Commander interrupted. He turned toward the biggest alien. "I'm afraid we'll have to make our introductions brief. I'm the Commander, Mr. Magnificent here is Gordy, this is Noah, and up there we have Jess. We were just about to make our departure, and it looks like we'll have to be taking you along. So if you'll be as quiet as possible and line up over there . . ." The Commander suddenly stopped talking as the littlest alien walked straight into Gordy and fell down.

"No, Ping, that's not where we line up," the biggest alien said as he helped the little one to stand up.

"Sorry about that, most inconvenient not having a head." The littlest alien sighed.

"But you can still talk?" Noah stepped back as Ping bounced off Gordy again.

"Ah yes, that seems to have been a miscalculation on my part, I'm afraid," said the biggest alien. "We're from the planet Saturn. When we charted this trip, I asked for life-form packages that would suit the planet earth, but somehow I must have miscalculated. I realize now that you don't talk through your feet on earth. Ah well, but I did get the optical centers right. You do see through your noses, don't you?"

Gordy burst out laughing.

"Hey, Commander, look, I can't see a thing!" he hooted, as he held his nose. Jess and Noah giggled, and even the Commander had to grin.

"Well, you didn't have it quite right, but you were close," the Commander answered.

"If we could only make contact with our mother ship, we could return to our own life forms. Until then, I'm afraid we'll just have to get by with these," the alien said as he flapped his arms. "I hope we won't be too much trouble for you. By the way, I'm called Forty-four, and this is Twenty-three, and this little fellow is Ping."

"More like Ping Pong," Gordy laughed, as Ping bounced off him again.

"Sorry, Mr. Magnificent," Ping apologized.

"You know, I'm beginning to like this kid," Gordy said as he pointed Ping in the other direction.

Suddenly everyone froze. From the aisle came the roar of the bus guard's voice. "Hey, Jess, where's Noah?" Jason Whitemore asked.

"Noah? Noah who?" Jess was trying to stall for time. "Oh, Noah, my brother Noah. Well,

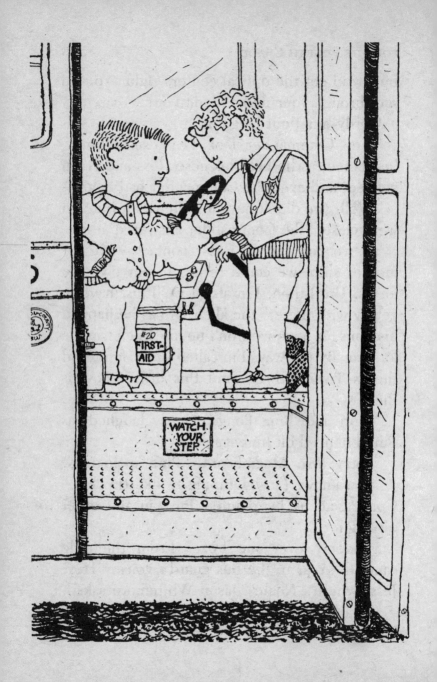

he got off already." Jess tried to sound as casual as he could. He reached down and carefully scooped everyone up and put them in his pocket.

"So what are you hiding in there?" Jason wanted to know, pointing to the bulge in Jess's pocket. Jason Whitemore had been a bus guard for the lasttwo years, and he treated all the other kids on the bus like possible criminals. His whole face lit up whenever he got to report someone to the office.

Jess laughed nervously and gently put his hand in his pocket, grazing the little heads (of everyone who had heads) with the tips of his fingers.

"Oh, these are just Noah's guys. You know how he takes them with him wherever he goes. He just forgot a few on the seat."

"Is he still playing with those little toys? Some fourth-grader. Does that kid ever plan on growing up?" Jason smirked as he got off the bus.

I don't know, Jess thought as he followed Jason down the bus steps. But if he does decide to grow up, I hope he waits till he's out of my pocket!

Chapter 7

When Jess got off the bus and hurried into Roosevelt School, he headed straight for the boys' bathroom. His heart was pounding so hard he was afraid someone in the hallway would hear it. When he ducked into the boys' room, he found an empty stall and closed the door. Carefully, he stuck his fingers into his pocket.

"It's OK, no one can see us," Jess whispered as he reached for the Commander and Noah. They in turn helped the two bigger aliens climb into Jess's hand, and Gordy followed with Ping on his back.

"Hey, Jess, how about letting us down. I think I'm getting airsick way up here!" Noah

42

yelled to his brother as he leaned on Jess's thumb.

"OK, we're going down," Jess whispered as he lowered them to the floor. It was a tile floor with lots of deep grooves, and the aliens kept falling into them.

"I think these guys are going to need some help," Gordy said, as Ping tripped and fell into 44, who tumbled into 23.

"Gordy's right," the Commander said. He helped 44 to his feet. "This terrain is too dangerous for the aliens without their eyesight."

"They can stay with you, Jess," Noah called up. "Just put them back in your jacket pocket. They'll be safe there."

"Excellent plan, Noah," the Commander agreed. He waved to Jess to come even closer.

"Noah's wish has certainly come true, at least part of it. The rest of the wish—the adventure—lies before us. We must all look on this as a mission, a mission to fulfill the wish so that things can return to normal," the Commander explained.

"I'll look after the aliens," Jess told him. "But what about you, Noah? Just what kind of adventure do you have in mind?" Jess looked down at his tiny brother, his face full of worry.

Noah knew that look well. Jess was known in their family as the Murphy to worry. He was always the first to hear strange noises at night, and Noah would often wake up to find Jess curled up beside him in the morning.

"Don't worry about me." Noah tried to reassure him. "I'm just taking the Commander and Gordy on a little tour. We'll be OK. We can see where we're going, you know."

"But, Noah, what if someone sees you? Or worse, what if they don't see you, and step on you?" Jess was beginning to panic.

"There is really no need to worry, Jess." The Commander sounded calm. "You forget that Gordy and I have been trained for danger. We've been in all kinds of situations, many of them much worse than this little excursion to the fourth grade."

Jess managed a smile as he thought about what the Commander had said. They were only going to the fourth grade, after all, and the Commander would be right there with Noah. Jess looked over at Gordy.

"Yeah, I'll be here to protect Noah, too," Gordy said.

"Look, Jess, all you have to do is drop us off at my classroom. We can meet you there at the end of the day. Our class gets out before yours does, so the room should be empty by the time you meet us," Noah told him.

Jess sighed. "OK," he said finally, "but be careful." He reached down and picked up the aliens, trying not to squeeze them too tightly. Just as he settled all three in his pocket, the boys' room door flew open, and Jason Whitemore walked in.

Suddenly Jess remembered that the stall doors didn't go all the way to the floor. They ended a foot above it. There was just enough space so that a person could bend down and look underneath. Jess instantly reached for a handful of toilet paper and threw it over Noah, the Commander, and Gordy. No sooner had the toilet paper engulfed the little figures in a sea of white than the large red face of Jason Whitemore appeared beneath the stall door.

"Hey, Jess, what's going on?" Jason asked as he twisted his head to look up at Jess.

Just then the toilet paper moved. Actually, Gordy sneezed. It was muffled by all the paper, but it did cause the paper to shake.

"What are you trying to hide in here, anyway?" Jason looked suspicious. "You're probably trying to sneak a mouse or a hamster into

school, just like Daniel Lipkin did last week. Well, there's only one way to find out for sure." Jason reached over and stuck his arm under the stall.

"Don't!" cried Jess.

"Why not? What are you hiding under there?" Jason wasn't giving up.

"Oh no, I'm sick. Really, Jason, I'm sick! Oh!" Jess groaned.

"Oh yeah? Well, just what kind of sick are you?" Jason sneered, reaching for the three tiny figures huddled under the toilet paper. It was at that moment that Jess did a truly brilliant thing. A truly magnificent thing, as Gordy would say later. Actually, Jess did the only thing that would stop Jason Whitemore from uncovering the toilet paper and discovering the three little comrades.

Jess took a deep breath, closed his eyes, and stuck his finger down his throat. Then he threw up all the potato chips he had just eaten on the bus.

"Oh, yuk!" yelled Jason shaking his arm, which had been in the direct line of Jess's attack. "Why didn't you say it was *that* kind of sick?" He backed away from the stall, groaning. After washing off his sleeve, Jason got out of the boys' room as fast as he could.

"Jess, you're a hero!" Gordy cried as Jess uncovered them.

"Yeah, I never thought I'd be thanking you for throwing up," said Noah. "It's not usually something you thank someone for. But I have to hand it to you, little brother. That was great!" Noah beamed.

Jess felt pretty good for someone who had just been sick. He had actually outsmarted Jason Whitemore, a fourth-grader. Before he could congratulate himself any further, the first bell rang.

Jess bent down to pick everyone up. He noticed the Commander signaling to him. He put his ear closer so that he could hear. The Commander was looking very serious.

"Now remember, Jess," the Commander said. "The aliens' safety is in your hands. Under no circumstances are they to leave your pocket. And whatever you do, don't let anyone see them. I don't want anyone getting too rough with them. They've lost enough body parts already."

"Don't worry, Commander, I'll take care of them." It was Jess's turn to be reassuring.

"What a wish," Jess mumbled to himself as

he gently placed everyone in his pocket and walked out of the bathroom. As he stood at the door to Mrs. Adams's classroom, he opened his pocket and whispered down, "OK, guys, prepare yourselves for the fourth grade!"

Chapter 8

When Jess opened the door to room 407, there was quite an uproar coming from the back of the room. Mrs. Adams was busy taking down the bulletin board display on the back wall.

"I'm going to let you decide on the theme for the month of October," she was telling the class. All heads were turned toward the bulletin board, and everyone was talking at once. It was the perfect time for Noah and his comrades to sneak into the room without being noticed. Jess quickly lowered them to the floor, just inside the door, and together the three little figures raced for the safety of the coat closet. Then Jess hurried along the hall to his classroom, with the aliens hanging on inside his jacket pocket.

"We'll be working on the bulletin board after lunch. Now I would like you all to get out your math books," Mrs. Adams said as she made her way to the front of the class. Her giant shoes passed by the half-open closet door, just as Noah peeked out.

"I never thought of Mrs. Adams's feet as being dangerous before," Noah whispered to the Commander. "But did you see the size of those things?"

Gordy let out a little laugh. "I like a woman with a big foot—shows she's sturdy."

"Well, there's nothing wrong with big feet as long as we're not under them," warned the Commander. "We've got to be extremely cautious from here on in. One wrong move and it could be our last," he added.

All three little figures took a step farther back into the shadows of the closet. They decided to sit down and take a rest while the class was busy with long division. Noah was quiet as he listened to the sounds his fellow classmates were making. He was amazed to discover just how noisy they all were. Jennifer Carnecilli was whispering to Maria Filona. Matthew Horochowski was humming under his breath. Shelly Pirozzi was throwing spitballs at the back of

Mark Carlton's head. John Bubs was at the pencil sharpener, loudly sharpening his pencil down to a stub. Suddenly Noah heard a new noise. It was the door to the classroom being opened, and then he heard what sounded like someone walking into the room.

"Nathan Cooper, this is the third Monday that you've arrived late to class this month. Just what do you have to say for yourself?" Mrs. Adams asked.

"Sorry, Mrs. Adams," Nate began. "When I went to sleep last night, things seemed to be all right. Then I had this dream—it was really mean. By the time I woke up . . ."

"Enough! Enough! We get the idea. You overslept again. Just take your seat. Since you are in such a poetic frame of mind today, you can lead our discussion on poetry this afternoon," Mrs. Adams told him.

"Oh great, I can hardly wait," Nate mumbled under his breath as he passed the coat closet on the way to his seat. Noah was about to call out to Nate as he walked by, but the Commander grabbed his arm and hurried him to the very back of the closet.

"Now's not the time for action. We'll just sit this out for a little while longer," the Commander told him. So together the three comrades sat back down and listened to the math lesson.

"Math is the one subject that could put me to sleep with my eyes open," Gordy complained. Even the Commander was getting restless. Noah sighed with relief when he heard Mrs. Adams ask everyone to hand in their papers. The three comrades skipped to the edge of the closet and looked over to see Mrs. Adams putting the homework assignment for the next day up on the blackboard.

"For tomorrow's homework, please finish page forty and do problems twenty through . . ."

Noah turned his attention from Mrs. Adams to Jason Whitemore, who was taking off his sneaker. Noah stared at the bottom of his foot.

"What's he doing?" asked the Commander.

"I think he's checking to see if he has a blister," said Noah.

Suddenly Nate reached over and grabbed the empty sneaker. He turned around and lifted it up, taking aim. Suddenly Noah realized that Nate was going to throw the sneaker directly at the coat closet!

Gordy and the Commander had just stepped

out of the closet and were leaning against the
giant door. When Noah saw the sneaker come
flying through the air, he raced out and tried to
warn them. But it came so fast that all three
were knocked to the floor as it hit the door with
a loud smack. Before they could get to their
feet, they heard Mrs. Adams's loud footsteps
approaching. Noah sat dazed, a few inches from
the giant sneaker. When Mrs. Adams bent
down to inspect it, she looked directly at Noah.
Noah was so shocked to see his towering teacher
stare into his eyes that he hiccuped.

Mrs. Adams let out a little screech. "Oh,
good grief, where did these mice come from?"
she moaned. "There must be a hole in this
closet, going down to the basement," she mumbled as she reached for the broom that was kept
in the corner.

The Commander grabbed one of Noah's arms,
and Gordy grabbed the other. Before he knew
it, Noah was being dragged through the open
door to the back of the closet again. He was still
in a daze. He couldn't believe it. Mrs. Adams
had looked directly at him, and all she could talk
about were mice!

"All right, the person wearing just one
sneaker please report to my desk," Mrs. Adams

commanded in her "that's it, you're in for trouble now" tone of voice. Jason hopped up to her desk, pointing and calling for Nate to come too.

"Sorry, Mrs. Adams, I guess I forgot for a minute that I was in school," said Nate, shuffling up to the front of the room.

"Well, Mr. Cooper, I've found that the best cure for such a memory lapse is an extra homework assignment. You do remember what extra homework assignments are, don't you?" Mrs. Adams asked.

Nate closed his eyes and sighed. "Yes, ma'am, I'm afraid I do."

Chapter 9

In the back of the closet the Commander and Gordy helped Noah to his feet. "That was a close call," the Commander said as he straightened Noah's jacket. "Are you all right?"

"Yeah, I guess so, but I don't get it," Noah whispered to the Commander. "Mrs. Adams looked right at me, and instead of seeing me she saw a mouse!"

The Commander just scratched his head. "I suppose it has something to do with being a grown-up. She saw you, but since this is all a wish-come-true kind of situation, she convinced herself that she didn't see you. Grown-ups have a hard time seeing magic in action, even though it's happening all the time."

"But why? If you can see magic when you're little, why can't you when you're grown up?" Noah wanted to know.

"I can't say for sure." The Commander sighed. "Somehow, grown-ups get all tangled up in paying bills and buying life insurance and worrying about getting caught in the rain without an umbrella, things like that."

"Whew! I'm glad I'm a toy," Gordy said. "Being a grown-up sounds horrible." He reached into his shirt pocket and pulled out his favorite purple yo-yo. As Gordy stood there, doing a number of complicated yo-yo maneuvers, Noah and the Commander turned to each other and smiled.

"I don't think we ever have to worry about you being a grown-up, Gordy!" The Commander laughed; then his face grew serious. "The grown-ups may not be able to see us, but everyone else can. Judging from the dangerous activities of some of your classmates, I suggest we stay hidden."

Just then, Tiffany Gasperetti opened one of the coat closet doors. She reached in and took her sweater off a hook. Gordy let out a warning whoop as he and the Commander and Noah went racing to the other side of the closet.

"Quick, climb up to the first shelf and hide behind the lunch boxes," yelled Noah. It was a narrow shelf, and they had to inch their way carefully along it so as not to fall off. They had almost reached Rachel Keck's hot pink Wonder Girl lunch box when Gordy remembered his yo-yo.

"Aw shoot, Commander. I forgot my yo-yo. I've gotta go back before someone steps on it," Gordy pleaded.

"Good grief, Gordy. How many times have I told you to keep your yo-yo in your pocket when you're on a mission?" The Commander shook his head while Gordy made his way around the lunch box and jumped to the floor.

"Don't let anyone see you, and get back here as fast as you can," the Commander called out. As Gordy ran toward the back of the closet, his little footsteps got fainter and fainter. Mrs. Adams's voice, meanwhile, got louder and louder.

"Nate Cooper, you will have no recess today," she was saying. "And Jason, go back and get your sneaker. Try and keep it *on* your foot, where it belongs!"

From the shelf, Noah watched Gordy as he passed a red boot on the way to his yo-yo. It had

rolled out the door and had landed beside
Jason's sneaker. As Gordy bent down to pick it
up, Jason Whitemore showed up to fetch his
sneaker.

"Hey! What was that?" Jason's voice roared
through the closet. He had caught a glimpse of
Gordy out of the corner of his eye. He knew he
had seen something, but he wasn't sure just
what it was. Meanwhile, Gordy was scrambling
toward the red boot. In seconds, Jason was
beside the boot and coming down hard on his
prey.

"I'll get you!" he said, as he rubbed his
sneaker into the floor.

"Help!" Gordy cried as Noah and the Commander hurried through the maze of lunch
boxes.

"I never should have let him go back alone!"
the Commander yelled as he raced through the
dark closet to try to rescue his friend. But
before he and Noah could get to the door, they
froze in their tracks. Two thunderous words
were ringing out of Jason's mouth. Noah had
never heard two more horrible words in his life.

"Squashed ya!" Jason yelled. The words filled
the closet and bounced off the walls as Jason
bent down to inspect what was lying under his

foot. Noah and the Commander peeked around a boot and saw Jason picking something up off the floor. Gordy's jacket sleeve hung limply from Jason's hand.

The Commander buried his head in his hands. Noah had never seen him so distraught. He had never imagined that the Commander could get upset. Suddenly, Noah realized that the Commander and Gordy wouldn't be a team anymore. Noah had always played with the two of them together. Even at Kramer's Toy Store the two little guys had stood together, side by side, on the shelf. It never occurred to Noah to buy one without the other. The Commander was calm and serious, while Gordy was goofy and lovable. It was unthinkable to imagine playing with one and not the other. And now suddenly the Commander was alone and looking lost. He had slumped to the floor, shaking his head.

"It's all my fault. It's all my fault!"

"Come on, Commander, you can't blame yourself." Noah tried to comfort him, but it was no use.

The Commander looked up. "Have you ever had a true friend? Not just any friend but a true friend?" He had a faraway look in his eye.

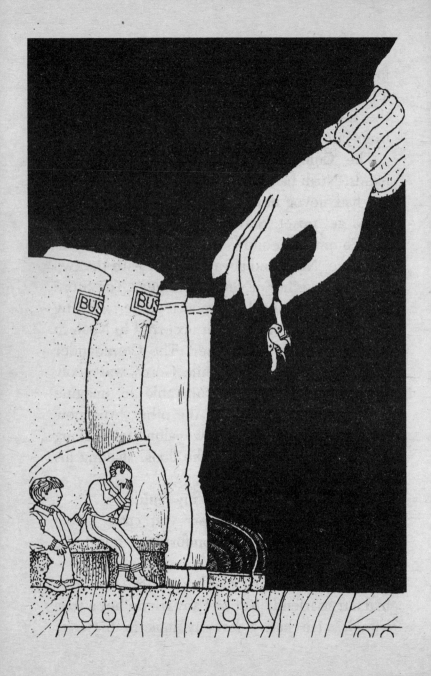

"Well, that was Gordy. My one true friend, always at my side, always there with a joke, with a smile . . ."

"And with a yo-yo!" came a familiar voice from behind a lunch box!

"And with a yo-yo." The Commander nodded. Suddenly, he lifted his head and grinned as Gordy came walking out from his hiding place.

"Well, I lost my jacket, but I still have my yo-yo!" Gordy said. "That was one determined fourth-grader. I knew he wouldn't be satisfied unless he stepped on something, so I pulled off my jacket and threw it behind the boot. He saw that and *bam!* That boy's got some big feet happening. Well, better he should do his stomping on my jacket than on my back. I got out of there in the nick of time. And look, I even managed to retrieve the old yo." Gordy grinned as he threw out his yo-yo for a spin.

"You're a sight for sore eyes!" the Commander said. "I have to admit, even your old ugly coconut shirt looks pretty darn good right now."

Noah stood smiling. So that's what he wears under his jacket, he thought to himself. Noah had never really imagined Gordy in anything other than his brown leather jacket.

"Yeah, that's a Gordy shirt, all right," Noah said, surveying the bright orange shirt that was covered with glaring green coconut trees.

"Glad to have you back, old friend!" said the Commander, giving Gordy a hug.

"Glad to be back, old friend!" Gordy hugged him back. Together they reached over for Noah, and the three little figures stood hugging, surrounded by boots and towering lunch boxes.

Chapter 10

Noah, the Commander, and Gordy had spent most of the morning hiding in the coat closet. After Gordy's narrow escape, the three little comrades decided to sit tight for a while. They hid behind a green and white dinosaur lunch box and tried to stay quiet. It was Gordy who jumped at the sound of Jason Whitemore's voice.

"Mrs. Adams, when I bring the attendance sheet to the office, should I tell them about Noah Murphy?" Jason was saying as he stood by Mrs. Adams's desk.

"Tell them what about Noah Murphy?" Mrs. Adams asked.

"Well, he came to school this morning, but he's not in class."

"Are you sure he came to school?"

"Oh yes, he was on my bus, and he got off just before I did. I talked to his brother. But he never made it to class. Something must have happened to him. Should I report him to the office?" Jason asked.

"Oh no!" moaned Noah in the closet.

"Oh yes. I suppose so," sighed Mrs. Adams.

The entire class started whispering as everyone wondered just what had become of Noah Murphy. There was one whisper that was louder than the others. It reached the closet just as Noah stuck his head out from behind the lunch box to listen.

"Your buddy Murphy is in for it now!" Jason sneered as he passed Nate Cooper's desk.

Noah stepped out in front of the lunch box, straining to hear Nate's reply. But Nate didn't say a word. He just took the rubber band he was chewing out of his mouth and aimed it at the back of Jason's neck. The next sound to reach the closet was a girl's loud scream. Nate was not the best shot with a rubber band, and instead of hitting Jason's neck he had hit Tiffany Gasperetti on the nose.

"Aw, shoot! I gotta practice my aim," Nate muttered under his breath.

Noah shook his head as he listened to Tiffany tearfully explain Nate's latest assault to Mrs. Adams.

"My nose! It feels like a giant bee just stung me on my nose. It was Nathan Cooper. He's the one that did it, Mrs. Adams. He shot me with a rubber band, and it feels just like a horrible bee sting."

Mrs. Adams told Tiffany to come up to her desk so she could take a look at her nose. "Mr. Cooper, I think you'd better come up too," Mrs. Adams commanded. Nate marched up to the front of the room amid a chorus of buzzing bee sounds from the other boys in the class.

All of this buzzing made Gordy let out a loud hoot of laughter, loud for someone four inches tall, that is. Noah and the Commander quickly reached over and covered his mouth with their hands. Fortunately, Tiffany was sobbing so loudly that no one was able to hear the little wisps of laughter coming from the closet. Noah and even the Commander were unable to control themselves. The three comrades were rolling about, holding their sides and trying not to

laugh. Just as they finally quieted down, Gordy
let out a giggle, and they all began again. It took
Mrs. Adams's stern words to quiet the entire
class—and those in the closet.

"That's enough noise. It's time to turn our
attention to social studies. And you may go to
the back of the room and stand in front of the
closet until you learn to behave, Mr. Cooper!"
Mrs. Adams pointed to the back of the room.

Noah couldn't see Nate, but he could hear his
slow shuffle coming toward the closet. Noah
grinned as he thought about Nate's theory
about the coat closet.

"You've got to look real tired. Let everything
sag," Nate had told him just the other day. "Sort
of slump back against the doors and close your
eyes. That way, Mrs. Adams will think that you
don't have enough energy to act bad anymore.
And she'll let you sit back down."

Noah, the Commander, and Gordy could
hear the loud rattle of one of the doors as Nate
slumped his shoulders against it. The other
door was still open, and the three comrades
made their way over to it.

"Just try and imagine yourself living in ancient Greece," Mrs. Adams was saying to the

class. "Just imagine what it would have been like."

Nate slumped down a little more.

Noah could just imagine what his friend was thinking. "Nate's probably imagining himself as the best shot with a rubber band in ancient Greece!" Noah whispered to Gordy.

"The way that kid shoots, it would take a lot of imagination to imagine that!" Gordy answered.

"Well, he may not be too good with a rubber band, but he's my best friend and the one person in this class who can help us," Noah said, looking over at the Commander.

"I don't think it's a good idea for too many people to find out about us, but since he's your best friend, I suppose it's all right. It was your wish, after all, that got us into this adventure. Just be careful out there," the Commander warned as Noah stepped from the closet. He scurried over to Nate and put his head all the way back so that he could look up at Nate's face. Nate's eyes were closed. Noah tried kicking Nate's high tops, but Nate didn't seem to feel it. Then Noah reached into his pocket and threw an old eraser at Nate's ankle. It was so tiny that

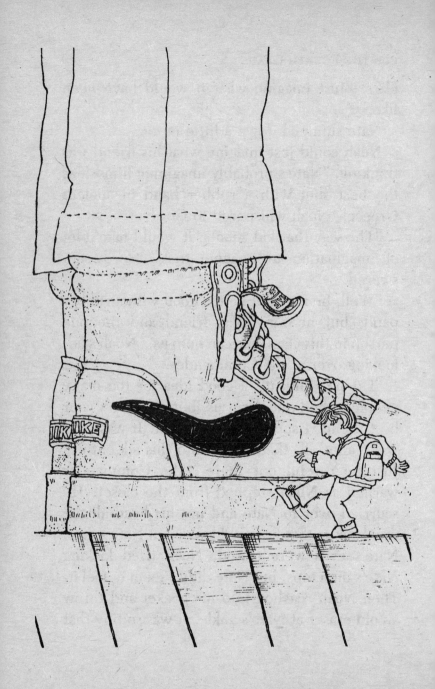

Nate didn't even notice. Noah was afraid someone else might hear him if he called too loudly, but he knew he'd have to risk it.

"Nate, can you hear me? It's me, Noah. Look down, will ya, Nate?" Noah was yelling as loud as he could.

Chapter 11

"That must be Tony starting up," Nate muttered as he listened to Noah's little squeaks.

Noah frowned. "Oh great! Now he thinks I'm Tony's stomach!"

Tony Morelli was the biggest boy in the fourth grade. He had a large and noisy stomach. Everyone sitting near him would look forward to social studies. Actually, it was Tony's serenading stomach that they looked forward to. Since social studies was the last subject before lunch, Tony's stomach would start gurgling just as they opened their books. Being good friends with Tony, Noah and Nate would usually sing along in whispers. Just last week, the trio had performed the entire first verse of *The Star*

Spangled Banner. The three even talked about cutting a record someday. They'd have to record in a studio at exactly 11:30, though, as that's when Tony's stomach was the most musical.

Nate looked up at the clock. "Gee, it's only a quarter after eleven," he mumbled. "Maybe that isn't Tony's stomach. It kind of sounds like a voice, a tiny voice." Nate slumped down a little further and listened.

"Nate, Nate it's me," Noah yelled with all his might.

Nate grinned. "Noah? What kind of stunt are you pulling? I can barely hear you. Where are you? Behind the coats?" Nate opened one of the closet doors just a crack and peeked in. "Noah, where are you? I can't see you," he whispered.

"Your sneaker," Noah yelled up to him.

"My sneaker? My sneaker's not in the coat closet. My sneaker's on my foot," Nate whispered back.

"I know, I'm trying to tell you that I'm on your sneaker that's on your foot!" came the faint reply.

"On my sneaker? That's on my foot— Agh!" Nate let out a cry of shock as he looked down at the little figure clinging to his high top.

"Mr. Cooper, did you have something to add

to this discussion?" Mrs. Adams called from the front of the room.

Noah stood shaking his head violently. Nate looked up at Mrs. Adams and then down at Noah and managed to croak, "No, Mrs. Adams, I don't think so. Sorry!" he apologized.

Noah was trying to get Nate's attention, but Nate was busy pinching himself. He closed his eyes tight.

"I'm dreaming, right? This is all a weird dream. So how come I don't wake up when I pinch myself?" He looked dazed.

"No, Nate. It's not a dream! It's real. I'm real. It's really me, Noah." Noah tried to sound as real as he could.

"But you . . . you're so short . . ." Nate whispered.

"That's because I've shrunk, Nate. I used this magic powder and wished myself this size," Noah tried to explain.

"But why? Why would you want to wish yourself that small?" Nate whispered in disbelief.

"So I could have an adventure with them." Noah pointed to the closet where Gordy and the Commander were leaning against one of the towering doors. The Commander smiled at Nate, and Gordy winked.

"Oh no!" Nate groaned. "Now I know I'm dreaming! That's the Commander over there, and Gordy just winked at me. Oh no! Mom! Mom! Wake me up, Mom! I'm dreaming—wake me up, Mom!" Nate began yelling.

"Nate, be quiet! Geeze, Nate, you don't need your mother. It's just me." Noah was trying to holler up to his groaning friend before everyone in the class heard him. And they probably would have heard him if there hadn't been so much noise coming from the front of the room. Noah held on to Nate's laces as he turned around to see what all the commotion was about.

Once again Mrs. Adams's class was in turmoil. This time it was all due to Tony Morelli and George Washington (George Washington was the class hamster). Tony had just gone up to the blackboard. As he passed George Washington's cage, his stomach had let out a loud, melodious gurgle. To George Washington, who had been happily dozing, it sounded like a volcano erupting.

The startled hamster was so frightened that

he threw himself against the cage, upsetting his water dish. The cage tipped dangerously over the edge of the table, then crashed to the floor. Noah looked on, horror-stricken, as George Washington came racing to the back of the room. Suddenly everyone in the classroom was yelling and screaming.

"Be careful, boys and girls. The mice might be back in that closet. Stay back, everyone!" Mrs. Adams called out.

Noah didn't know what to do. Suddenly he saw the Commander and Gordy come racing from the open closet door. Noah leaned over and helped them climb up on Nate's high top. Nate stood staring, wide-eyed, too dazed to move.

"Quick, climb in there!" the Commander shouted, as he pushed Noah up and into the cuff of Nate's pant leg. Then the Commander helped Gordy up and was about to climb in after him when Nate suddenly stepped back. The Commander was thrown over the sneaker and landed on the floor.

"Get up! Get up, Commander!" Gordy and Noah yelled to their fallen comrade. But the Commander was too dizzy to stand.

"Oh no! The Commander's not going to make

it!" Noah yelled as he watched George Washington race toward the closet. He and Gordy looked up to see the towering figures of his classmates heading for the dazed Commander.

"Stay here, little buddy. You'll be safe, don't worry," Gordy shouted to Noah, bolting out of the cuff and jumping to the floor.

Gordy reached the Commander just in time to see the oversize hamster come sliding around the last desk. As Noah watched in horror, the Commander and Gordy disappeared into the coat closet with the monstrous George Washington squealing hungrily behind them.

While everyone came rushing to the back of the room to look for the runaway hamster, Nate made his way to the front, near the blackboard, so he could be alone. He bent down and carefully opened the cuff of his jeans and looked in. On seeing the miniature version of his best friend he gasped and almost fell backward. Nate tried taking deep breaths as he stared down at Noah's tiny body. "It's not a dream, is it? You're still here!" he whispered to his friend.

"I'm still here, but Gordy and the Commander won't be if we don't do something. George Washington could swallow them whole!" Noah moaned.

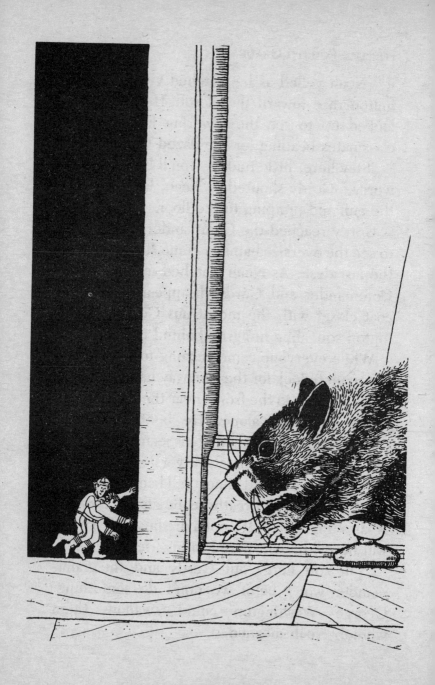

"Oh my gosh, you're right!" Nate was coming back to life now that he realized he wasn't asleep. He gently picked Noah up and put him in his shirt pocket, where he'd accidentally dropped a freshly chewed wad of gum a few minutes earlier.

"Nate, help! I'm stuck to all this gum!" Noah tried to wiggle himself free, but his sneakers were stuck fast. The whole pocket reeked of the sickening sweet watermelon scent. Watermelon flavor was Nate's favorite flavor. Nate reached in and pulled Noah off the bright gum.

"At least it's sugarless," he said, laughing. "Your feet won't get any cavities."

But Noah wasn't laughing. He was too worried about Gordy and the Commander.

When Nate looked down at the serious face of his friend, he stopped smiling. "I'll go and see if I can get them out of there," he whispered as he put Noah back in his pocket and stuck the gum to the bottom of a desk.

"All right, class, everyone please return to your seats," Mrs. Adams was saying. "Since I did see a mouse in the closet this morning, I don't think we should open the closet doors until I've called a janitor." Then she closed the doors tight.

"George Washington is twice the size of the mouse, so I'm sure he'll be all right. Tiffany, you go to the office and request a janitor to come at once. Now, let's get back to our studies. Where were we? Oh yes, ancient Greece."

"Ancient Greece! Who can think about ancient Greece at a time like this?" Noah moaned as he slumped down against the warm soft flannel of Nate's shirt. He could hear the loud thumping of his friend's heart, and the scent of watermelon was overpowering.

Chapter 12

Together Nate and Noah sat dismally, thinking about the fate of the doomed Commander and Gordy. If they could only find a way to distract Mrs. Adams and get back to the closet before the janitor arrived or before the hungry hamster found his lunch.

"I've got it," Noah called up to Nate. "You're cold, Nate. You need your sweatshirt."

"No, I don't," Nate whispered, his head bent down over his shirt pocket. "I've got a flannel shirt on, and besides it's warm in here."

"No, you're not really cold, dummy! But if you tell Mrs. Adams that you need your sweat-shirt, we can get back to the closet and save the

Commander and Gordy," Noah explained impatiently.

"Oh yeah, good thinking," Nate muttered as he raised his hand to try to get Mrs. Adams's attention.

But something else had caught Mrs. Adams's attention. It was Jason Whitemore. He had just returned from the office and was standing in the doorway, looking as if he'd seen a ghost. He stumbled into the classroom and stood mumbling next to Mrs. Adams's desk.

"They had no heads. There were these little green bodies with no heads. And they were holding these tiny belly buttons." His voice trailed off to a whimper as the entire class burst out laughing.

"Now, Jason, try and calm down. What are you talking about?" Mrs. Adams asked as she put her hand on Jason's shoulder.

"In the hallway, Mrs. Adams. They're out there. I saw them. They were running down the hall, and they didn't have any heads!" Jason suddenly seemed to be gasping for air.

"Jason, you're getting yourself into a state. There's probably a logical explanation for what you saw or thought you saw. I think we'd better let the nurse have a look at you." Mrs. Adams took one of Jason's hands in hers and headed for the door. She turned to give some last-minute instructions.

"Tony Morelli, I'm leaving you in charge. Everyone please read chapters five and six. I'll be right back. And Mr. Morelli, see that everyone remains quiet until I return," she called over her shoulder as she quickly rushed Jason out the door.

The minute she was gone, the class was in an uproar. Everyone was laughing and talking about Jason's "headless bodies." Even Tony, who had been left in charge, couldn't resist laughing when Danny Rush ran up to the blackboard and began drawing lots of little headless bodies with giant belly buttons. Everyone thought it was funny. Everyone except Noah.

"Oh no! They must have gotten out of Jess's pocket!" Noah called up to Nate.

"Who got out of Jess's pocket?" Nate asked.

"The aliens! Remember the aliens I had with me the other day at your house? Well, when I made the wish, some of the magic powder got on them and they came to life on the bus, with the Commander and Gordy. Oh my gosh, Nate, the Commander and Gordy are in trouble, and we're sitting here talking!"

Nate's hand went up in the air like a shot, but Tony was busy getting Danny to sit back down.

"If you don't stay in your seat, Danny, I'm going to report you to Mrs. Adams," Tony threatened. Danny finally returned to his seat, and Tony looked in Nate's direction.

"Tony, may I get my sweatshirt out of the coat closet?" Nate asked.

"And just how do we ask, Mr. Cooper?" Tony rubbed a piece of chalk between his chubby hands, the way Mrs. Adams did when she stood at the blackboard.

Noah sat in Nate's pocket, fuming. "Of all the times for Tony to start acting like a nerd!" he mumbled under his breath. Nate, meanwhile, gritted his teeth and managed to smile.

"Dear Mr. Morelli, may I please have permission to go to the coat closet?" Nate asked as sweetly as he could.

"That's much better, Mr. Cooper." Tony grinned. "But gee, Nate, I don't know. Mrs. Adams said we were to keep the doors closed until the janitor came."

"Oh, come on, Tony, I'll just get my sweatshirt and close the doors right up," Nate pleaded.

"Oh well, all right, but hurry," Tony said,

sitting down in Mrs. Adams's chair. He jumped back up when David Fry threw a paper airplane at his stomach.

"Nate, hurry! Before we're too late!" Noah called up to his friend.

But when they reached the coat closet and opened the doors, they were horrified to find that it *was* too late. Noah stood up, so he could look over the edge of Nate's pocket. He could see George Washington sitting in the closet, contentedly licking his paws, the way he always did after a meal. Noah crouched down as Nate reached over to get hold of the hamster. Nate held him up and tried to look into his mouth, but the squirming ball of fur would have none of it. He squeezed himself right out of Nate's hand and went tumbling onto a lunch bag. Nate quickly cupped his hands over him, and George Washington had to admit defeat. He finally quieted down in Nate's hand.

Noah looked out from the pocket. "Oh, Nate, look at him. He looks fatter, doesn't he?"

"Well, he always looks fat," Nate answered, trying to be optimistic.

"But he has a weird look on his face, like he has indigestion or something. Don't you think he has a weird look on his face?" Noah moaned.

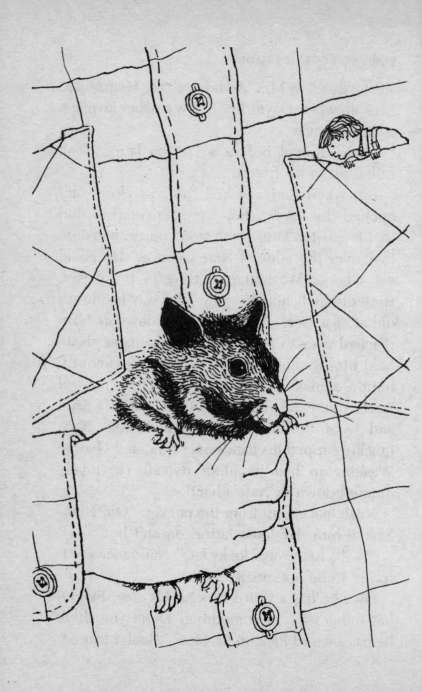

"Yeah, but hamsters always have a weird look on their faces when you catch them. He's probably just mad that he can't go racing around anymore. Quick, get down, here comes Tony."

Nate handed the indignant hamster to Tony, who had come to the back of the room. While Tony carried George Washington back to his cage, Nate searched the closet. Suddenly Nate gasped and bent down.

"Oh no!" he groaned.

"What? What did you find?" Noah called up frantically from the pocket.

"Just this," said Nate, as he gently poked a tiny scrap of material into the pocket, next to Noah. Noah felt the tears welling up in his eyes as he picked up the little tattered shreds of bright orange material with green coconut trees on it. Noah sank back down in the pocket.

"I don't believe it! I won't! They can't be dead! They can't!" he whispered as he held the material up to his cheek. "They always make it! No matter what, they never die!"

He closed his eyes as the tears fell to his cheeks. Deep down he knew that this was real life. Just as Gordy and the Commander had been able to come alive, it was also now possible for them to die. They weren't toys anymore.

"This was the worst wish I ever made. And I don't know how to undo it. What have I done! What have I done!" Noah whispered into the empty pocket.

Chapter 13

Noah was still slumped down in Nate's pocket when he suddenly felt Nate walking.

"Where are you going, Nate?" he cried up to his friend. "We've got to stay and find the Commander and Gordy. We can't give up!" But before Noah could finish, he heard a familiar voice and knew immediately why Nate had returned to his seat.

"All right, class, I'm back. You can all settle down," Mrs. Adams exclaimed as she walked in the door. "We certainly haven't gotten much work done this morning. Let's just hope things go better this afternoon. Oh, did George Washington come back?" she asked, looking over to the hamster's cage. "Well, that's a relief." Mrs.

Adams sank down into her chair with a sigh.

"But what about Jason?" Tiffany wanted to know.

"Well, our nurse, Miss Berlee, seems to think that he may have had a reaction to his allergy medication. You know Jason and that overactive imagination of his. If the medication was causing blurry vision, Jason *could* have imagined that he was seeing all sorts of things. I'm sure he'll be fine once he's rested for a bit in Miss Berlee's office. All right, everyone, let's get our lunches from the closet and line up at the door."

Noah held onto the little strings inside Nate's shirt pocket to steady himself as Nate raced back to the closet. He was the first one there and the last to leave. Nate searched everywhere for the Commander and Gordy, but they were nowhere to be found. Reluctantly, Nate grabbed his lunch bag and joined the others in line. As he walked past George Washington's cage, he glared at the overweight hamster, who hiccuped in reply.

I'll never pet another hamster as long as I live, thought Noah glumly. He fluffed up a bit of lint from the bottom of the pocket and put it behind his head for a pillow.

Mrs. Adams was so glad that things were returning to normal that she forgot all about the fact that Noah was absent. "Everyone, please be quiet as we walk to the cafeteria," she almost sang.

Noah stayed low in Nate's pocket as Nate walked with the rest of the class out into the hall. But it was hard for Noah to stay put. He kept wanting to stand up and look over the edge of the pocket for Jess and the aliens. He was beginning to worry that something had happened to them, too. But there were so many kids in the hall, he didn't dare stand up. As they walked through the cafeteria doors, Nate moved to the side and suddenly stopped. He bent his head down, held his hand over his mouth, and excitedly whispered into his pocket, "I just saw two of the aliens!"

"Where?" Noah cried, as he sprang up in the pocket.

"They ran into the kitchen. They were running along the wall. Geeze, they looked weird. It was one thing to see them as toys, but alive they are definitely the strangest things I've ever seen! No wonder Jason was so freaked out!" Nate shook his head.

"Nate, listen. We've got to get them out of

there before they get hurt. They can't see where they're going."

"I know that, Noah, but they went in the kitchen. How are we supposed to get them out of there? Kids aren't allowed in the kitchen, remember? If anybody saw us in there, we'd be in big trouble," Nate whispered back.

"They would see you but they wouldn't see me. I'm not exactly a regular-size kid, anymore. I'll go into the kitchen and get them out and meet you back here." Noah yelled as loud as he could. The noise in the cafeteria was becoming deafening, as three other classes filed in. "Find a place where you can let me out," Noah called up to Nate.

"Hold on," Nate told him as he began to walk toward the trash cans. He bent down and pretended to tie the laces on his sneakers. But he didn't reach into his pocket. He just kept tying and untying his laces.

"Nate, what are you doing? Come on! Get me out of here!" Noah cried excitedly.

"Noah, I can't. This is crazy. It's too danger-ous. Someone might step on you. Forget about the aliens. They were just toys, anyway." Nate tried to reason with him.

"That's right, they *were* just toys, but they're

alive now. Just like you and me! Oh, come on, Nate, you know how I feel about my guys. I can't just leave them in there. You're my best friend, Nate, and I'm asking for your help, please . . ."

"OK, OK, I'll help, but let's check our watches and meet back here in twenty minutes, with or without the aliens. You promise me you'll be here?"

"I knew I could count on you, Nate." Noah smiled as he looked at his watch. "It's five after twelve, now. I'll meet you back here at twelve twenty-five, right behind this trash can."

"OK," Nate whispered as he reached into his pocket. Noah grabbed onto his fingers, and Nate pulled him out. Then Nate held him in his hand for a minute. "You're sure you want to do this?" he asked.

"Sure I'm sure. It'll be OK. I'll come back here with the aliens." Noah tried to sound brave. He hoped Nate wouldn't notice just how shaky his voice had become or how his knees were beginning to wobble.

"Take care of yourself," Nate called down as he lowered his hand to the floor and opened it beside the trash can. Noah quickly jumped off and raced for the wall. Everyone in the cafeteria

was busy finding a table or standing in line for hot lunches. No one even noticed the little figure that dashed along the bright blue wall and disappeared into the kitchen.

Noah never knew he could run so fast. When he got to the kitchen, he didn't know which way to turn. The room seemed immense. He ran around a corner and was almost stepped on by the dishwasher. He quickly found a low shelf and climbed up to safety. He sank down exhausted, leaning against a large kettle. He knew he couldn't rest for long. Nate would be waiting. But the thought of leaving the safety of the shelf filled Noah with fear.

It's like being in the land of the giants, he thought as he watched a kitchen worker walk by. She threw a wad of tinfoil at the trash can but missed. The tinfoil went crashing down to the floor like a giant meteorite falling from the sky.

"Maybe Nate was right. Maybe this is too crazy," Noah mumbled to himself, looking down at the mountain of tinfoil below. "How am I ever going to find them?" he wondered. Leaning over the shelf, all he could see were massive ankles in giant shoes coming down hard on the linoleum floor. There were no aliens in sight.

Chapter 14

Noah took a deep breath and climbed down from the shelf. The coast seemed to be clear. The kitchen workers were all busy getting lunch ready. But which way should he go? He had started for the corner to his left when he suddenly heard the aliens. He recognized their tiny squeaks immediately. They seemed to be coming from the cabinet to his right. He turned around and raced along the edge of the bottom shelf.

"Oh my gosh! How did you get up there?" he gasped. For there in front of him were 23 and 44, wailing away on top of the giant work boot of the dishwasher.

"Forty-four, Twenty-three, don't panic! I'm

right below you," Noah yelled to them as loud as he dared. There was so much noise in the kitchen, the frightened aliens couldn't even hear him.

"OK, I know what I have to do; I have to stay calm," Noah told himself.

He took another deep breath. "The Commander would tell me to stay calm, and Gordy would tell me to be brave. But I'm having a hard time doing either without them," Noah moaned. Then he bit down on his lip as he grabbed hold of the giant boot that stood in front of him and began the long climb up. But the dishwasher's boot wasn't very clean, and Noah kept sliding on patches of greasy dirt.

"Can you hear me? It's me—Noah! I'm going to get you down!" he yelled to the aliens as he reached the top.

"Noah! Yes, we hear you!" 44 cried out as he extended his arms in Noah's direction. Noah grabbed hold of his hands and then reached for 23. Together the three little figures held onto each other, and for a moment none of them was able to speak. Noah was the first to say anything.

"Where's Ping?" he asked as he tried to steady himself by holding onto the laces of the work boot.

"We've lost him!" 44 cried out above the roar of the crashing plates and silverware. "It's a long story, but we got separated from Jess, and then we lost Ping."

"Don't worry, we'll find him. For now we have to worry about getting . . ." But Noah never finished his sentence for at that moment the dishwasher had looked down.

"Ugh! Mice!" he yelled as he shook his leg wildly. Things happened so quickly then that the entire kitchen was thrown into turmoil. All of the women were either screaming or yelling out orders on how to catch the mice. Meanwhile, the dishwasher had run for the broom. Everyone in the kitchen was now sure that there were mice, but no one knew just where.

When the dishwasher shook his leg, he had brought his boot up in the air. Noah had been holding onto the laces, and the aliens had been holding onto each other. All of a sudden they were thrown high up into space.

Heights were the one thing Noah really hated. Sailing across the kitchen, he felt himself turning as green as the aliens. Suddenly he was going down, and he closed his eyes tight, expecting the worst. But it was a soft landing for he had fallen into a bin of dirty dish towels.

As soon as Noah was able to sit up without feeling dizzy, he began to look around for the aliens. He leaned over the bin and wondered where they could be. Suddenly, he spied them on the counter just to his left. They stood trembling under a huge lettuce leaf that matched their skin color almost perfectly. Before Noah had a chance to call out to them, a kitchen worker swept her hand across the counter. In one quick sweep all of the little bits of lettuce and the two aliens who were hiding under them were gone.

"Oh no!" cried Noah as he watched the worker empty all of the little bits from the counter into a large stainless steel bowl. Then she took a bottle of salad dressing and poured it on the lettuce. As Noah watched her carry the bowl over to the lunch line, he let out a little gasp.

I'll never be able to get them out of this. And it's all my fault. First my dog eats off their heads and now . . . But he stopped himself in mid-thought.

"I have to be positive and think like the Commander. They won't be eaten! I'll get them out of this somehow," he mumbled as he began to climb out of the bin. Fortunately, it was quite close to the floor, close for a person of normal height, that is. It was still dangerous for someone only four inches high.

The bin's plastic legs were just the right size for Noah to wrap himself around. As he began to inch his way down, he felt like a fireman going down a fire pole. But the idea of sliding down that terrifying distance to the floor made his hands sweat. He was afraid he'd fall off if he slid too fast, so he kept grabbing the middle section of the bin to steady himself. He'd slide a bit and then stop. It seemed to take forever, and each time he stopped, he would look over anxiously at the lunch line.

"Boy, am I starved," Tony Morelli bellowed from the lunch line.

When Noah heard Tony's voice, his heart seemed to stop. That means they'll start scooping out the food, he thought as he desperately tried to slide farther down the bin. He knew that Tony Morelli was always the first one in the lunch line. Lunch was the high point of Tony's day. Noah could hear Tony's mother, who worked in the lunch line, talking to Tony as she filled his plate.

"Only half a piece of bread today, Tony," she said, nodding to his tray. Noah cringed as he heard her add, "But you can have an extra helping of salad. Now be a good boy and eat all your greens."

44 and 23 must be on Tony's plate, Noah reasoned, as he slid faster and faster down to the floor. They were dropped right on top of the bowl, and the stuff right on top went on Tony's plate. Please don't eat my aliens, Tony! Please!

Noah finally reached the floor, just after the dishwasher walked past. The dishwasher was certain the mice had gotten behind the refrigerator, and he was trying to find some mouse traps to put behind it. All of the other lunch ladies were too busy serving lunch to worry about the mouse problem anymore. As soon as he was sure the coast was clear, Noah began running along the bottom of the cabinets. He dashed over to the wall and across the room, heading for the doors that opened into the cafeteria.

He was running as fast as he could. He knew every second counted. He knew how fast Tony Morelli could eat.

Suddenly he stopped, just inches away from the doorway. He looked down at his watch and groaned. It was only 12:13. Nate wouldn't be waiting by the cans until 12:25. Tony could eat all of his lunch and half of Nate's by that time!

He couldn't believe how little time had passed since he had first entered the kitchen. It had seemed like forever to him. He now stood listening to the deafening roar coming from the cafeteria. It was filled with all of the fourth- and fifth-graders in Roosevelt School. There were even two third-grade classes having their lunch. Noah knew that without Nate he could never find Tony's table in time.

Since there was nothing else he could do, he decided to head toward the trash cans and wait for Nate there, as planned. He waited for all of the sneakers to pass, then raced out from the wall.

He had almost reached the cans when he realized that someone was behind him, right behind him. And it was someone very, very big. He could feel the vibrations on the floor and hear the horrifying sounds of giant sneakers pounding the linoleum. He couldn't bring himself to look behind him. He was afraid he wouldn't be able to go forward if he did. If he could just keep running. He was *so* close to the trash cans, just a foot or two away.

That's when he fell. He tripped over a straw someone had thrown from a nearby table. It was lying just in front of the can, and it sent Noah falling over his feet. He landed hard on the floor, flat on his face. The last thing he heard was the loud crash of a sneaker coming down next to his ear. He felt his whole body go rigid as he waited for the huge mass of rubber to come smashing down on him.

Noah had often thought of death and all of the different ways you could die, but he had never imagined it would be like this. He closed his eyes tight as his whole life flashed before him, and then he saw his tombstone:

HERE LIES NOAH MURPHY
STEPPED ON BY A
LOWLY THIRD-GRADER

He didn't know if it was a third-grader behind him, but the way his luck was going it probably was. Somehow the thought of being pulverized by a third-grader was worse than the thought of being pulverized by a fourth- or fifth-grader. Either way he just hoped it would be quick. He held his breath. He waited. He took another breath. He waited.

Chapter 15

"Are you OK? Are you hurt? Are you taking a nap, or what?" The thunderous whisper filled Noah with relief. He opened his eyes and looked up at the towering figure of his best friend.

"Nate, what are you doing here? It isn't twelve twenty-five yet!"

"You know me, I'm never on time. And in this case I figured you'd rather see me early than late. To tell you the truth, I haven't been able to touch my lunch. I kept running back and forth to this trash can to see if you had shown up yet. Boy, I'm glad to see you!" Nate was kneeling down, pretending to tie his sneaker. "But what happened to the aliens? Didn't you

see them?" he asked as he lifted Noah gently in
his hand.

"You're not going to believe this, Nate, but I
think Tony's about to eat them!" Noah said.
"They got thrown into a bowl of salad, and it's
kind of a long story. I don't have time to explain
it all. We've just got to get to Tony before he
gets to his salad because I think that's where the
aliens are!"

Nate cupped his hand over Noah and put him
in his shirt pocket. Then he ran back to his
table. He and Noah and Tony always sat together at lunch. As Nate reached the table, he
saw Tony looking down at his plate of salad and
frowning.

"You call this lunch? One measly piece of
roast beef and a mountain of green stuff. It looks
like something George Washington would have
for lunch." Tony groaned.

Noah thought about Gordy and the Commander. He prayed that they hadn't ended up
as George Washington's lunch. Then he remembered 44 and 23, and his spirits lifted as he
heard Tony say, "Hey, Nate, you like salad.
Have you got anything good to trade?"

"Yeah, I could really go for a salad today."

Nate sat down quickly and reached for his lunch bag.

"What happened, your sister make your lunch again this morning?" Tony grinned as he pointed to Nate's untouched lunch bag.

Noah knew that Nate and his sister Allison took turns making lunches in the morning. Whenever Allison made Nate's lunch, it was usually something weird. Allison loved to experiment with food. Nate usually threw away his sister's concoctions and just ate the fruit.

"How about an apple? It's really red and that means it's juicy." Nate reached in his bag and grabbed the apple that was on top.

"Oh, come on, Nate. Can't you do better than that?" said Tony. "I might as well keep my salad. There's more to it than that little apple, and if I put ketchup on the cucumbers, I can pretend they're french fries." Tony picked up his fork and began to poke at the lettuce on the edge of his plate.

"Wait!" cried Nate, jumping out of his seat. Noah almost went flying out of his pocket. "You haven't tried Allison's new tofu burger!" Nate yelled. He started to put his hand back in his bag, but Tony stopped him.

"If that's all you've got, don't bother. You can't pawn off Allison's funky food on me. You forget, I've seen her tofu burgers! I don't know how she gets them that disgusting green color, but you can bet they're not going to get any-where near my stomach. I'll stick with this hamster food, thanks!" He looked back down at his plate.

"You know how boring salad is!" Nate almost screamed. "Why don't you take my apple? You can find someone to trade with. I'll bet someone will give you a piece of bread or a bag of Cheezos for it. Remember what we learned in health? Apples are natural tooth brushes. Lots of kids would want a natural tooth brush," Nate pleaded.

"OK, OK, I'll trade, already. Just save me some of those french fries," Tony said, pointing to the cucumbers in the salad. He took the apple and left the table.

Nate waited and watched Tony go up to a table of third-graders. That's when the salad began making all the noise. It wasn't a loud noise, just a few squeaks. Noah recognized the alien dis-tress call right away. He called up to Nate, who had heard the little cries too. Then he stood up so he could see what was happening.

Poking through Tony's salad with his finger, Nate suddenly let out a laugh. 44 was wedged between two tomato slices, and 23 was stuck with his back end in a cucumber slice. They looked so strange and funny. Their bodies were oily green, and their little arms and legs were wiggling to get free. Where 44's head should have been there was a radish. And 23 had a blob of French dressing above his neck. Nate was awestruck and amused at the same time. He just sat and stared, unable to touch them.

"Come on, Nate," Noah urged. "Pick them up quick!"

But it was too late. Tony had come back to the table.

"Doesn't anyone around here care about their teeth?" Tony moaned as he bit into the apple and sat back down. Noah crouched lower in Nate's pocket.

"What happened? Didn't anyone want to trade?" Nate nervously eyed Tony's salad.

"Naw, nobody thinks your natural tooth brush here is anything special. How come you're not eating the salad? You want what's left of the apple back?"

"No! I want the salad. I just got to talking to somebody, and I haven't had a chance to eat.

HOT LUNCH

TODAY
CHEESE DOG
   CHILI OPTIONAL OR
   TURKEY FRANKS
BUTTERED MIX VEGS.
SLICED PINEAPPLE
PEANUTS
MILK
TOMORROW
PIZZA
BUTTERED CORN
ICE JUICES MILK
PRETZEL ROD

NATE

Look, you can have all the cucumbers. Why don't you go get some ketchup for them?" Nate picked out the cucumbers and almost threw them at Tony.

"Ketchup, what would my life be without you!" Tony sang as he walked over to the hot lunch counter with the cucumbers in his hand.

As soon as Tony was gone, Nate scooped up the aliens and dropped them into his pocket alongside Noah. He tore off a little bit of napkin and put that in too. The aliens squeaked with relief at hearing Noah's voice.

"It's all right. You're safe now," Noah told them as he wiped the salad dressing off 23. At first the aliens were too upset to talk. Noah tried to calm them down by patting their backs.

44 was the first to speak. "We've got to find Ping," he cried.

"How did you become separated from him?" Noah asked.

"We were all together in the jacket," 44 began. "Then Jess put us in his shirt pocket. We spent a long time there, and then Jess had to go to a place called gym. He was afraid that we might get hurt and told us that we'd be safe in his desk until he got back."

"That desk place was so horrible!" 23 interrupted.

"Yes, I have to tell you it was a nightmare. There were all kinds of weird and strange things in there, even for an alien," 44 sighed.

"The way it smelled," 23 groaned. "We've been to a lot of planets, and believe me, there is no place in this galaxy that smells that bad."

Noah couldn't help but smile at this. He knew how Jess loved to save things. The last time his parents had gone to open house they discovered Jess's desk full of "an incredible assortment of treasures," as his father had kindly put it. There were old jelly beans, stones, bits of chalk and crayons, a matchbox filled with string, pieces of an old salami sandwich, bits of moss that had dried out, parts of a mini race car, and a pickle wrapped in tissue. Noah could certainly sympathize with the aliens. But he still wanted to know how they had become separated. "What happened next?" he asked.

"Jess had left the desk wedged open with a book so that we would get some air. I knew we'd have to be patient and wait for him to return. We tried to convince Ping to just lie down and try to sleep, but the smell of the place was so strong it was very difficult. Finally 23 and I were able to doze off, and we assumed Ping was doing the same. But when we woke up, he wasn't at my side. You see Ping is very young and very curious. He loves to explore. We wandered through the desk, reaching out and calling for him. Finally, we heard him somewhere above us. I reached out and felt a rope. Ping called down to us. He told us that he had found the rope, tied his shoe around it, and had thrown it up and over the edge of the desk. I told him to come back down and wait for Jess to return, and that's when we heard him drop. He must have lost his footing and fallen from the edge of the desk." 44's shoulders went limp as he remembered the horrifying sounds of Ping's cries for help.

23 continued: "We searched for another rope, and when we found one, we attached my shoe to it and threw it over the edge. It took a while but we finally made it to the top."

"That's when we heard this terrible ringing noise," 44 added. "It was so loud and so startling, we both lost our balance and fell from the edge, just like Ping."

"That must have been the bell," Noah told him. "It just lets us know that the first lunch period has started."

"How uncivilized," murmured 44.

"Go on, what happened next? Didn't you get hurt?" Noah wanted to know.

"We landed on a smooth flat surface. I assume it was Jess's chair. We weren't hurt, since internally we're aliens and not humans, no bones to speak of, you see. Ping was gone. He didn't answer our calls, and so we decided to search for him. It took us a long time to climb down the chair, and when we reached the floor, I knew our chances of finding Ping were very slim," 44 sighed. "But where are the Commander and Gordy?" he asked.

Noah explained how they had gotten separated.

"If only our fellow comrades were with us." 23 sank further down in the pocket after hearing of the fate of the Commander and Gordy. Together the three little figures grew quiet as they thought of their missing friends.

Noah shook his head and tried not to cry. "I never imagined the fourth grade could be such a dangerous place," he whispered, almost to himself. "I just didn't know." His voice trailed off. The three sat in silence, lost in their thoughts.

Chapter 16

Noah, 44, and 23 spent the remainder of the lunch period in Nate's pocket. As the bell signaling the end of lunch rang, Nate and Tony stood up to go.

"Hang on," Nate whispered beneath his breath to Noah and the aliens. "We're going back to the classroom."

"Hey, Nate, you forgot to toss your tofu!" Tony said.

"Oh yeah." Nate absentmindedly picked up his lunch bag and walked over to the trash cans. But as he tossed it into the sea of colored garbage, he noticed a tiny string coming out of the bottom of his lunch bag. And attached to the string was what looked like a little purple yo-yo.

Nate reached back in the trash for his bag and held it up, looking at the tiny yo-yo dangling from the bottom.

Where did that come from? he wondered as he opened the bag.

"Oh my gosh!" His loud whisper echoed through the bag. He smiled down at the Commander and Gordy. "How did you get here?" he gasped. "Never mind, you can tell me later," he said quickly as he pushed the bag into his shirt. He walked as fast as he could up to Mrs. Adams, who was waiting outside the cafeteria.

"Mrs. Adams, may I please go to the boys' room?" Nate asked.

"Is it urgent, Mr. Cooper?" Mrs. Adams sighed.

"Yes, Mrs. Adams, it is definitely urgent!" Nate said emphatically.

"All right, just meet us back at the room," Mrs. Adams told him.

Nate tried not to run, but he was so excited over finding the Commander and Gordy that he almost skipped down the hall. That's when he bumped into Jess, who was on his way to the cafeteria. If it had been any other day, Jess would have been laughing and talking with his friends on his way to lunch, but he was doing neither today. In fact, he looked downright miserable.

If only I hadn't left my desk open, Jess was thinking as he walked down the hall; the aliens would have been safe and sound right now, and I could have kept my promise to the Commander and Noah. His thoughts were suddenly interrupted as Nate reached over and grabbed his arm.

"It's about your brother," Nate whispered as he pointed to the boys' room. Nate had such an anxious look on his face that Jess decided he'd better see what Nate wanted. Jess went up to his teacher and asked permission to go to the boys' room.

Nate, meanwhile, went into the bathroom and checked all of the stalls. He wanted to be sure the boys' room was empty. Then he reached in his pocket and gently lifted out Noah, 44, and 23.

"Wait until you see the surprise I have for you." Nate grinned at his best friend as he lowered him to the counter. Noah couldn't imagine what Nate was talking about.

They made a strange little trio, standing

there next to the sink. Noah was in the middle,
with a headless alien hanging onto each of his
arms. The aliens were so terrified of getting lost
again that they were holding on for dear life.
Together the three small figures looked up to
see Nate pull out his lunch bag from inside his
shirt.

"Oh, thanks, Nate. But I really don't want
anything to eat right now," Noah sighed.

"Oh, I think you'll want what I have for you in
this bag," Nate told him. He put the bag down
on the counter and reached inside.

"Nate, really I'm not in the mood for any of
Allison's weird tofu or whatever else you have
in that . . ." Before he could finish, Nate had
lifted Gordy and the Commander from the bag
and put them on the counter alongside Noah
and the aliens. At that moment, Jess walked in,
and when he saw 44 and 23 standing next to
Noah, he grinned with relief. Nate told Jess to
stand with his back to the door, in case anyone
tried to come in. Noah, the Commander,
Gordy, and the aliens were all laughing and
talking at once.

"You're alive! You're alive!" Noah was yelling
at the top of his lungs. Gordy had him in a
friendly head lock. "But your shirt—we found

your shirt!" Noah reached into his own pocket and brought out the little scrap of material with coconut trees on it.

"No way was I going to let that ball of funky fur get my favorite shirt!" Gordy said as he let go of Noah and smoothed out the front of his shirt.

"Uh, um . . ." The Commander was motioning for Gordy to show them his back.

"Well, OK, maybe he got a little! But the most important part is still on me!" Gordy grinned as he turned around. The entire group burst out laughing as they looked at Gordy, for the hamster had ripped off the entire back of his shirt. Everyone was laughing and talking at once. They were so relieved to be together that they forgot for a moment about their missing comrade.

"Hey, where's the little Ping Pong?" Gordy finally asked when everyone had quieted down.

"It's all my fault. I should never have gone to sleep," 44 sighed.

"No, it's all my fault!" Jess burst out.

"Your fault? What do you mean, Jess?" Noah walked over to the edge of the counter and looked up at his little brother. Jess explained how he had left the aliens in his desk.

"It's OK, Jess. Forty-four told us all about it." Noah tried to comfort him. "It wasn't your fault. Leaving the desk open a crack was really good thinking. The aliens do have to breathe." Noah suddenly turned to 44. "Just how do you breathe?" he asked.

"With these bodies we breathe through our belly buttons," 44 explained. "You see, that's why it was so difficult being in Jess's—how shall I say—aromatic desk. Our sense of smell seems to be extremely heightened. Jess had told us that when he returned from gym he would take us with him to the cafeteria for lunch. When we failed to locate Ping, we decided to try and get to the cafeteria and find Jess. We just let our belly buttons guide us there. Your lunchroom has some powerful scents coming from it."

"Yeah, I think the food stinks too." Nate smirked.

"Hey, if Forty-four and Twenty-three found their way to the cafeteria by their sense of smell, maybe Ping did the same thing," Jess cried.

"That's excellent logic, my friend," said the Commander.

"But even if he did make it to the cafeteria, I

don't see how we could find him there, now," Nate said softly.

"By this time, hundreds of sneakers have pounded on that floor," Noah added. "It would be a miracle if he made it through alive."

"Miracles were how this whole adventure got started," the Commander reminded him.

"You know we can't give up on the little guy." Gordy looked around at his comrades on the counter. No one said anything, but Noah knew in his heart that they would have to try to find Ping.

"OK, it's settled then. We get back to the cafeteria as fast as we can to find him," Noah said.

"Now, just hold on," the Commander commanded. "It's important that we all stay together so no one else gets lost. Nate, may we all ride in your pockets till the end of the day?"

"Sure," Nate whispered.

"Thanks, Nate. I'm glad we can depend on you. You have a true friend here," the Commander added, looking from Nate to Noah.

"Now, we must all remain in Nate's pockets while Jess and Nate search for Ping," the Commander instructed over the protests of 44 and 23.

"I'm sorry." He turned to 44. "I know you want to help in the search, but it's just too dangerous for any of us out there. We'd be more help to Ping right now sitting safely in Nate's pockets, not causing any more problems. Nate and Jess are better equipped to find him. They're a lot taller, and they have their heads. Believe me, it's the best plan for everyone." The Commander put his hand on 44's slumped shoulder. Then he looked up at Jess and winked.

Jess instantly bent down, his face just above the little headless body.

"Don't worry, Forty-four," Jess whispered. "I'm on my way to the cafeteria right now. I'll spend my whole lunch period looking for him. I ate the best part of my lunch on the bus, anyway. So I'll have lots of time to look for him. I'll find him, Forty-four, really I will!" Jess lifted him from the counter and handed him to Nate. After Nate had put Noah and the Commander and Gordy in one pocket, he put the aliens in the other. Then he and Jess left the boys' room.

"If only I had closed my desk, or taken them with me to gym, none of this would have happened," Jess said as he and Nate walked down the hall. They were almost to the cafeteria when Mr. Kibbles, the principal, stopped them.

"Nathan Cooper, aren't you heading in the wrong direction? Didn't I just see your class leaving the cafeteria?"

"Oh . . . Oh yeah! I mean yes! Yes sir!" Nate fumbled and stumbled and finally turned himself around. He reluctantly headed back to his classroom. Mr. Kibbles turned to Jess.

"And you, young man, aren't you the younger Murphy boy? Jess, isn't it?"

"Ah yes . . . Jess Murphy, sir." Jess smiled faintly. "I was just on my way to lunch, Mr. Kibbles. See ya," he began, heading for the cafeteria, but Mr. Kibbles called after him.

"Murphy! Jess Murphy! Now I know why I had you Murphys on my mind today. It seems Miss Berlee found a book order envelope with your name on it this morning. You'd better go over to her office right now and pick it up."

"But I was just on my way to. . ." Jess tried to turn to the cafeteria, but Mr. Kibbles put his hand on Jess's shoulder and turned him in the direction of the nurse's office.

"Go on. You'll have plenty of time for lunch. Book orders are a student's responsibility, and you have to learn to be less careless with your responsibilities," he added firmly.

"Darn that Miss Berlee!" Jess moaned under his breath. Now I'll have to waste all this time getting a stupid book order, he thought as he walked farther and farther away from the cafeteria. I'll never be able to keep my promise to 44, he worried; I'll never find Ping!

Chapter 17

The first person Jess saw when he walked into Miss Berlee's office was Jason Whitemore. Jason was lying on the couch. He looked up curiously at Jess, and Jess returned the look.

"Don't you feel good, Jason?" Jess asked.

"I'm OK." Jason looked at the wall. Then he turned back to Jess. "It was just my medication. It was too strong, or something. I started seeing things. Miss Berlee says it can make things look different. Like ordinary things can look really weird," Jason tried to explain. "But they were so little and so real, and they had no heads," Jason murmured to himself.

Jess realized that Jason must have seen the aliens. He wondered if he had seen Ping. "After you saw these weird little things together, did you see any of them by themselves?" he asked.

"No. There were two of them. Why? What do you know about them?" Jason looked suspiciously at Jess.

"Oh, nothing. It was probably just dust that you saw," Jess offered. "Once when I was watching this piece of dust in class, I looked at it so hard that it began to look like a person. It began to look like Mr. Kibbles. Only it was Mr. Kibbles with a tail!"

Jason smiled. He was glad there was someone else in the office to talk to. Miss Berlee had gone to the art room to see about some third-grader whose hand was stuck in a paint jar.

"I guess it could have been a piece of dust or something," said Jason. "Hey, I forgot why I was going to the office in the first place. Didn't you tell me that your brother was on the bus this morning?" Jason suddenly sat up. He swung his legs over the side of the couch.

That's when Ping let out a squeak. It was so loud that even Jason heard it. He looked down to see the little green body dancing wildly around his shoe. Jason was trying not to believe his eyes.

"You're just dust! Just a little thing I'm

imagining. It's that crazy medication. You're just an old piece of dust!" Jason whispered as he looked down at Ping through squinting eyes.

"Were you talking to me?" Jess asked, coming over from Miss Berlee's desk.

But Jason didn't look up at him.

"Just dust. You're just dust!" he kept whispering in a shrill voice.

Ping stood still, just below the couch. This earthling was insulting him! "Who are you calling a piece of dust?" Ping shrieked.

"Oh no! Now it's talking! Miss Berlee, it's talking! The dust is talking!" Jason swung his legs back up onto the couch and dove under the blanket to hide.

Jess rushed over to the couch and stood over Ping. He was so relieved to see the little alien that he forgot Jason was there.

"Ping!" Jess cried out as he picked up the little alien and quickly placed him in his shirt pocket.

"Ping?" Jason poked his head out from under the blanket.

"Ohh . . . Jason, you look terrible. You better lie back down and rest," Jess said, as he fluffed Jason's pillow for him.

"Murphy, tell me, did you see the talking

dust with the big belly button? Ping? You said
Ping! Why did you say Ping?" Jason started to
babble as Miss Berlee walked back into the
office.

"No, no, Jason. I said I'm so happy I could
sing now that I've found my book order." Jess
grinned as he picked up his order envelope
from the desk. He turned to Miss Berlee and
shook his head.

"Sick boy there, Miss Berlee. That's one sick
boy!" Jess whispered as he rolled his eyes to the
ceiling.

Out in the hall he looked down in his pocket.
"Are you OK?" he whispered to Ping.

"I'm OK. I'm just a little tired," Ping answered.

"You must be exhausted. I have the feeling
you've been running around in circles since you
got out of my desk," Jess said.

The tiny figure in his pocket made no reply.
Jess pulled his pocket open wider. As he looked
down at the tiny slumped figure, Jess began to
laugh.

"What's so funny?" a fifth-grader asked him
as he came down the hall.

"Nothing, nothing." Jess couldn't stop grin-
ning. "It's just that I have this alien snoring in

my pocket!" he said under his breath. The exhausted Ping had fallen fast asleep, and Jess could hear the tiniest alien snores coming from between his little green toes.

As he passed Mrs. Adams's classroom, Jess flashed a thumbs-up signal to Nate, who was standing at the blackboard. Seeing the wide grin on Jess's face, Nate knew at once the impossible had been possible after all. Thanks to a miracle that they'd all hoped for, Jess had found Ping. A little cheer went up in Nate's pockets as he related the news.

Mrs. Adams looked up from her desk. Nate was standing next to the hamster's cage, and the hamster could hear the faint cheers of joy coming from Nate's pockets. The disgruntled hamster began squealing angrily.

"Why, George Washington, whatever is the matter with you? You sound downright angry!" said Mrs. Adams.

Just as Nate walked past the cage to return to his seat, Gordy hung out of the pocket for an instant.

"So long, fur face! It's been fun," he called, as he blew the humiliated hamster a kiss.

Chapter 18

When they were all finally huddled together on the back seat of the bus for the ride home, the little figures suddenly grew quiet. Nate and Jess sat on either side of them, keeping a lookout.

Gordy finally broke the silence. "Boy, that's one adventure I'll never forget." They all shook their heads in agreement, while the little aliens swayed back and forth. But no one could speak because they were all thinking the same sad thoughts. They had known it wouldn't last, that it wasn't meant to, as the Commander had explained. But somehow they had gotten so caught up with looking out for each other, they had forgotten that it was just a wish—a wish that had brought them together and a wish that wouldn't last.

Now they would all have to return to the normal world (the world where Noah was four feet three inches tall, not four inches). And a world where Gordy and the Commander and 44 and 23 and Ping were all just brightly colored toys lying in a shoe box.

"It's only logical to assume that now that our adventure is over and we've returned to our starting point, your wish is all used up," the Commander finally said to Noah in a low voice.

Noah couldn't bring himself to look up. He knew what the Commander was trying to tell him, that they should be saying good-bye while they still could, while they were still real. But when he gazed into those steady blue eyes of the Commander's, Noah couldn't find the words. He quickly turned to 44 and reached out for his little green hand.

"I wanted to tell you, I'm sorry about your head and all. I should have kept you off the ground, where Overdue couldn't reach you. I'll be sure to take better care of you when . . . when . . ." But he was unable to finish, to say "when you're just a toy again."

"It was quite an experience for us," 44 answered warmly. "Your fourth grade seemed like a planet all its own. Actually, it was a lot like the planet Froton, though I must tell you Froton smells much better." 44 reached out, and Noah hugged him good-bye.

Next Noah stepped up to 23. He started to shake his hand but stopped when he saw that it still had salad dressing on it.

"We can't have you traveling around the universe looking like some tossed salad!" Noah laughed as he wiped off the French dressing with the tail of his shirt.

Before he could turn to Ping, the littlest alien came bouncing off the Commander and landed in Gordy's arms.

"Now, Ping Pong, you've got to learn to settle down." Gordy chuckled as he took off his hat and gently placed it where Ping's head should have been.

"You can wear this for luck," he said as Ping bounced in his arms. "But if you want to get back to Saturn, you'll have to behave yourself and stay out of trouble." Gordy tried to sound firm, but somehow he couldn't quite manage it.

"They *are* getting back to Saturn, aren't they?" Gordy turned to Noah with a wink.

Noah wiped away a tear and winked back.

"Oh sure," he said. "They've got the whole galaxy to explore." Noah tried to smile.

"And what about us? What adventures do you have in mind for the old Commander and me?" Gordy asked.

"Well, I . . . I . . ." Noah was looking up at Gordy's lovable and goofy face. So lovable and so real that Noah felt as if his heart were breaking.

"I don't want you to change back. I want you to stay just the way you are, real! I want you to stay real!" he blurted out. "Why can't the wish be forever?" He buried his head in Gordy's crazy coconut shirt.

"Aw, come on, little buddy, nothing lasts forever, and besides, you wouldn't want it to. You wouldn't want to be four inches high forever. You know Jess was right: we are awfully short for the fourth grade, aren't we?"

"Yeah, I guess so," Noah said softly.

"It's all changing, you know. Changing all the time. And that's what's so great about this world of ours, even for a toy," Gordy told him. "Come on, now, how about a hug for your Mr. Mighty Magnificent?"

As Noah reached up to put his arms around

his mighty friend, his eyes filled with tears again.

"Hey, hey, you're raining on my coconuts!" Gordy protested, as he pretended to brush Noah's tears from his shirt.

Everyone laughed at this, even Noah.

"Now let's shake like the big guys." Gordy tried to sound firm again.

As Noah held out his hand, he felt Gordy press something into his palm. When he looked down, he saw the old beat-up purple yo-yo.

"For luck, little buddy, for luck," Gordy whispered.

Noah squeezed the yo-yo and tried to smile. When he finally turned to the Commander, he shook his head.

"I saved you for last because . . . because . . ."

But he never got to finish what he wanted to say, for just at that moment the bus hit the bump on Black's Hill, and everyone went flying in the air. For an instant everything went black. Noah felt himself spinning and falling as he came back down on the seat. All four feet three inches had landed, and he knew it the minute his feet hit the floor.

With a sick feeling in his stomach, he looked down at the seat and saw Gordy and the Commander lying beside him. Their little warm bodies had turned back into the stiff, cold plastic they had always been. Even their smiles had become unreal, frozen on their faces.

Jess and Nate were jumping up and down excitedly, patting Noah on the back. Nate bent down and picked up the aliens, who had gone flying onto the floor. Their bodies were as hard and stiff as they were when Noah had first bought them. Gordy's hat had turned to hard plastic and was stuck fast to the top of Ping's neck.

Noah quietly picked up the Commander and gently placed him in his hand. It was hard to believe that just seconds ago the two had been standing side by side. Noah extended the Commander's little arm and put the tiny hand in his, as if to shake it.

"I didn't get to say good-bye, Commander! I didn't get to tell you. I saved you for last because . . . because you were the hardest one to say good-bye to. You've always been so brave and good and strong—just the way I wish I could be. I never got to tell you how much you've meant to me."

He clasped the little figure to his chest and closed his eyes as they filled with tears.

"I should have told you. I should have told you . . ." he whispered as the school bus pulled up in front of the Murphy house.

Chapter 19

Noah and Jess walked down the bus steps in silence. But as they reached the curb, they suddenly stopped. There was quite a commotion coming from the bus. And it seemed to be coming from the back seat.

"Noah, Noah, wait!" It was Nate. He had opened a bus window and was yelling at the top of his lungs—two things that you were definitely not supposed to do on a school bus. As Noah and Jess stood at the curb, they were amazed to see Nate do something that was guaranteed to get him into trouble. He actually leaned out the window and then threw something at Noah. It looked like Jess's potato chip bag from that morning. Before one of the bus guards was able

to grab his arm and escort him to the front of the
bus, Nate managed to call out to Noah.

"Look inside! I found it under the seat! But
Noah, this time, wait for me. . . !" His voice
trailed off as the bus pulled away.

Noah bent down and picked up the potato
chip bag. When he turned it over, a little pouch
dropped out into his hand. Both he and Jess
recognized it at once. It was the pouch from the
magic kit.

"Is it empty? Is it empty?" Jess wanted to
know.

"Yeah, it's half empty," Noah said as he held
it up to the light. "And half full!" He grinned as
he squeezed the tiny yo-yo in his other hand.